CROWN PRINCESS ACADEMY

BOOK ONE

USA TODAY BESTSELLING AUTHOR

A.J. FLOWERS

To Lexi C. Foss for encouraging me to follow my passion and cheering me on through a rough pregnancy and delivery. To my husband for supporting a new mom and her writing dreams. This book has a little piece of my heart in it. Thank you for helping it come to life.

To all the princesses

This is one crown you don't want.

Born and raised in the Dregs, the last thing I expected was the "honor" of being recruited to Crown Princess Academy.

And by honor, I mean fighting for my life against the fae that rule our world.

Our first exam is in three weeks and not every student will make it out alive… don't these bimbos realize that? I'm not fooled. I know how ruthless the fae can be.

All the princess initiates are captivated by Lucas, the sexy fae Crown Prince who, in turn, seems fixated on *me*. He can't know that I'm actually the most powerful Malice Caster in the Dregs. I'm sure my talents for the Criminal Guild won't earn me any extra credit in my princess classes.

All my life I've stayed one step ahead of the two-faced fae and their Malice, the out of control black magic that has nearly wiped out all of humanity. This is my chance to do more than survive—this is my chance to fight back.

I'll play the Crown Prince's game. I'll wear the tiny initiate crown, dance in my glittering pink dress, survive the deadly exams, and ultimately graduate as the Crown Princess all while he thinks I'm playing right into his plans.

He's in for a surprise when I reveal who I am and wipe that sexy, smug grin off his face... I just hope my heart doesn't forget he's the enemy.

Crown Princess Academy: Book 1 is the first of a planned trilogy. As it is a series, there will be a cliffhanger. This is an upper YA/NA paranormal and fantasy series with enemies-to-lovers romance and HEA.

CHAPTER ONE

LUCAS

*H*oly Fae, this place was a slum.

Not that I expected the Dregs to be glamorous. The human slums skirted the Kingdom's border like a cauterized wound that refused to heal. I knew it would be bad, but seeing it for myself gave me a whole new perspective.

I must have been gaping at the rundown hovels and broken excuses for civilians who wandered the streets, because the human who'd brought me here chuckled on a rasp.

"Take it in, stranger," said my overpriced guide, a man with a long scar that ran through a silver iris and past his jawline. He glanced at me with his working eye where a spark of mischief gleamed.

"You're in the Northern Sector now. Guildmaster Gavin don't take kindly to trespassers, so you best stay close to me."

I tugged my cowl around my face and nodded. The fabric strained against my pointed ears that I'd managed to stuff underneath a tight band around my head. Nothing would stand out more in the Dregs than a fae, much less the Crown Prince. If I was discovered, my plan would be ruined before it even began.

I was here for one reason.

Redemption for my people.

I clutched a splintered box to my chest that held the key to my farfetched hopes. The artifact inside was intended for one worthy of the task. There was one candidate, but I hadn't expected her to be here.

According to my magic, she would be a woman of grace, power, and prestige that would be strong enough to stand up to my fellow fae.

Now that I saw the Dregs for myself...

Surely this is a mistake.

"This way," the human said, his voice gruff as his boots splashed through mud puddles. He gave me a raised brow. "Might want to rough up your clothes if you plan on fittin' in."

I looked down at my buckled boots, cursing that

I hadn't thought about that. How many Dreg-dwellers had adornments on their boots? By the hungry looks I was getting from the local riffraff, not many.

Bending down, I popped off the brass bands and tossed them behind me. Shadows billowed out of hidden corners to pounce on the trinkets and I hurried to follow my guide deeper into the bowels of this horrid place. I was already here. Might as well see my crazy plan through.

"Stay close and keep those teeth of yours hidden," my guide hissed. I hadn't realized my canines had extended—a defense mechanism when I was in danger. The fangs betrayed me as fae and I wrapped my lips over the sharp points, willing them to recede. "You're paying me the other half when we get there," he continued. "Don't want to lose you to some Malice Casters that spot easy prey or a wealthy ransom."

I nodded my curt agreement. Although, if a Malice Caster tried to make a go at me, they'd be in for a rude surprise.

The buildings crowded in on us and leaned like nightmares peering down ready to devour a fae stupid enough to leave the Kingdom. I glanced up at the shuttered windows, spotting flashes of metal that could have been decorations...

Or crossbows.

It wasn't hard to spot the Guild, the one building that stood upright without scaffolding to hold it in place. Ancient gothic spires marked the home as a Malice Den, a place where humans had captured and tamed the vile blackness that had destroyed so many of them.

One such human stood at the ready, guarding the entrance. A female, I realized, in the lithe way she moved, but my eyes couldn't track her easily. Shadows whispered around her, dulling her details and making her look more like a figment of my imagination than a Guild's guard.

"Malice Caster," my guide hissed. "Give me the creeps, they do."

The female he referred to held my attention far better than anything else in this pit. I was accustomed to magic and it swirled effortlessly around her with controlled waves, distorting the light so that I couldn't make out her face.

Whoever she was, she was talented, and by the looks of it far better trained than half of the fae back home who didn't appreciate their magic. It came naturally to fae. We didn't have to work for our gifts.

Not this caster. She ran her fingers through the inky blackness, coaxing it, communing with it. I recognized the strained relationship she had with her magic.

She'd suffered for this. Now she owned her power and the flare of confidence in her dark eyes said she dared me to test her on it.

Maybe the Dregs weren't so bad after all, not if they produced females like this.

She tilted her head, pressing one hand to her ear as if listening to a whisper, then nodded.

"Gavin is expecting you." Her words came out magically distorted, frustrating me that she wouldn't show me who she was or even let me hear her true voice.

I watched her as she moved, graceful enough to rival a fae, and I couldn't resist expending a sliver of my Light magic to allow me to see through the Malice she wrapped around herself like a protective shield.

A leather bodice fitted to her sleek form and her hair bunched at her neck, practical, out of the way, but with a push of my own power I spotted its golden gleam underneath the layers of inky shadow. A blonde rogue would stand out, so it was no wonder she kept herself hidden. Her face, as much as

5

I wished to see it, remained a mystery. She kept an extra layer of magic to distort my view and when she glanced at me, I dropped my efforts and clutched the box tighter to my chest.

"Inside," she snapped, and I stiffened.

No one ever ordered me around.

Instinct told me to teach this Caster a lesson, but she thought I was a rogue trader, a thief—one of them.

Ducking my head, I walked inside and my guide shuffled in after me, no doubt driven only by the promise of payment. I wasn't going to give him a single drop of my power until I saw the Guildmaster.

The Caster took us through dark hallways, skipping the main entrance hall that seemed reserved for black market trades that would never be tolerated on the other side of the border. I glimpsed several groups crouched over tables and cringed when I noted an unconscious body on the ground. The armor said they'd captured a fae... I should intervene, but I had a task to do.

The body didn't glow, didn't exude any life-force or energy.

Nothing I could do for the dead.

Rotten Dreg-dwellers...

The Malice Caster seemed unaffected by the nearby trades with morbidly questionable goods and took us up an endless flight of stairs. My guide heaved, breathless, by the time we got to the top. The Caster glanced at me and I wondered what she was thinking until I realized I hadn't shown any sign of exertion, so I filled my chest with a long breath.

I could have sworn she rolled her eyes.

She snapped her fingers and shadows opened the doors. "Make it quick," she snapped.

Another order.

Then she abandoned us in a puff of smoke, leaving me to match gazes with the overdressed ex-Elite waiting behind a desk, his fingers steepled and a smug grin on his face.

Guildmaster Gavin De'Lorn.

My guide inched closer to me. "Can you pay me now? I, uh, best be gettin' on."

Rolling my eyes, I dug into my cloak pocket and extracted the bag of light crystals. When I'd been in the Fae Realm I could produce them at will. Now, I had a finite supply of the precious gems. "Here," I said as I shoved the pouch at him.

He fumbled for it, tugged the loop to peer inside and then grinned, his yellowed teeth making a brief appearance before he resumed his scowl. "Pleasure doing business," he said with a nod and then scurried out of sight.

I clutched at the box again. The artifact inside burned with my last hope.

Magic, don't fail me now.

2

PENNE

"Who the Malice was that?" I snapped, not having time for Gavin's games right now. Either he had a job for me, or I needed to get back to the Breeder Nest where Jilly was waiting. My heart twisted thinking of her going without dinner for two nights in a row. Breeder offspring were meant to be kept alive—not comfortable. I was the only reason she got regular meals and I didn't have time for this muck.

The Guildmaster smirked at me from behind his desk and twisted a splintered box into my view. "Who sold me the package is unimportant. What you should be asking is, do you want this job or not?"

Crossing my arms, I dropped my shadows enough so he could see my scowl. "We both know

that if you want a job done right, I'm your best girl."
After six years of doing Gavin's dirty work starting
at the ripe age of twelve, I had more experience than
anyone in the guild. I was in my prime, eighteen and
stronger than ever in commanding the Malice that
lurked in my chest.

It earned me enough coin to feed myself and a
few Dreg-dwellers who had no one else to count on,
Jilly being my latest attempt at charity and friendship that would likely end just as well as the others.

Never stop trying, came a male's voice that origi-
nated somewhere in my head. He didn't talk to me
often, but when he did, it came with a sleek, velvety
sensation and left a metallic tang in my mouth. So
much so that I'd dubbed him "Steel."

"Shut it, Steel," I whispered under my breath.
Having as much Malice as I did meant I was knee-
deep in crazy.

Gavin ignored my mumbling and pushed the box
closer to me. "True, you are my best girl, which is
why I called you here tonight. I need this delivered
to the Malice Caster Academy… undetected."

My scowl deepened. "Why discretion? I can walk
into the Academy any time I want." If this wasn't a
job that was going to pay out, he was wasting my
time. There were three corrupt merchants in the

Northern Sector tonight and I'd rather take a few treasures off their hands than play Gavin's games.

"You don't even know what's in the box," he said, his smirk growing as he twisted the cube again.

I knew better than to ask. "Deliveries" often had something to do with the fae, and when it came to the fae, payouts would be good, which was the only reason I was still standing in Gavin's oversized office.

Yet, it still didn't make much sense. I'd been within earshot to hear the stranger's short conversation with Gavin. Whatever was in that box needed to get to the Malice Caster Academy and Gavin could have picked any Malice Caster under his command to do the job—ones that were much cheaper than me.

"You know how I feel about the Academy," I said, hoping to push the offer higher if there was some danger involved, which knowing Gavin, there would be.

That's a good girl, you don't work for free.

Glad to know Steel approved. Yet, I preferred not to go back to the Academy where I'd grown up, where I'd been a star student and plucked at an early age because of my Malice scar. I rubbed at the hidden mark underneath my tunic that rested

11

directly over my heart. Few children were born with the blemish, and even fewer survived it into adulthood, but those that did... that's precisely why Malice Academy had bought me from my overeager mother who'd likely drooled at the bounty on my head. It was probably enough for her to leave the Dregs altogether, so I never expected to see her again.

A familiar bitterness swelled in my chest. Sold as a child to a bunch of black magic casters in exchange for finery and decadence, what kind of woman did that?

Don't be so quick to judge, a delicate voice said in my mind, this one female.

Like I said, knee-deep in crazy.

I glanced at my black magic pixie, a conjuration of my relationship with Malice that had been with me as long as I could remember. This voice had a body associated with it. She flitted in and out of the inky shadows that drifted from my hair as she giggled. She was pretty, in her own way, a sharp little chin and rosy cheeks on her otherwise dark skin. She always kept her hair up in a glittering headband of onyx jewels that matched her eyes.

"Go away, Zizi," I said under my breath, absently swatting at her. She giggled again and flitted her glittering wings, deftly zipping out of the way of my half-hearted attempt to smack her. If I didn't have time for Gavin's nonsense, I certainly didn't have time for a pixie's ramblings.

Gavin frowned. He couldn't see my pixie and probably thought I was missing a few daggers from my belt, if you know what I mean, but he tolerated my conversations with Zizi. I was valuable. And when it came to valuables, Gavin hoarded them in his little castle in the Dregs.

I just hoped he never figured out how much I needed him. His influence gave me the freedom to explore the Dregs. Every now and then he gave me a mission that sent me into the Kingdom with enough coin to bribe the guards in the event I had a stow-away or two.

I'm getting you out of this Malice-infested hole, Jilly, just you wait.

"This delivery isn't going to Malice Academy," he said, grinning with a set of pearly whites few in the Dregs could boast. "You're going to the Kingdom."

What?!

I dismissed my Malice with a flick of my wrist before he spotted how that news excited me. My shadows seemed to have a mind of their own when my emotions fluctuated. "But the job—"

"This job will pay three times the bounty," he said, that glimmer sparking in his eyes whenever he talked about a big payoff. "I have a client at the Rose Academy House that will pay handsomely for this delivery and I need to make sure it gets there." He got up and leaned onto his knuckles, making his desk creak. "Can I count on you, Penelope?"

I hated it when he called me that.

Conjuring my shadows to mask my face again to hide my smile, Zizi bounced with excitement around Gavin's head and Steel offered an encouraging chuckle.

"Consider it done."

***

IT DIDN'T NORMALLY BOTHER me that Gavin would break a deal. The box snuggled against my hip held something of extreme value. Even if I could appreciate value, I feared its origin would make it more trouble than it was worth.

The stranger who'd brought the artifact to Gavin hadn't been a Dreg-dweller, that much I was certain of. His clothes had been too clean, the layer of Dreg on him faint above otherwise perfect threadbare that would have sold for a decent price on the streets. His movements, too, had me on edge. Too confident, and his eyes, peering at me with such intense curiosity beneath that cowl had set every Malice-alarm in my skin on edge.

Could he have been a fae?

Perhaps.

Why don't you open the box? Zizi offered, flitting around my head and leaving a trail of inky Malice in her wake.

"That sounds like a terrible idea," I grumbled, keeping my voice low and muffled by magic as I stalked through the dark streets.

Or a wonderful idea, Steel offered.

Zizi huffed her disappointment and batted long eyelashes at me. She pretended she couldn't hear Steel, but I got the sense that she could. *Pleeeeease? I hate not knowing!*

Ignoring her, I took a sharp left and then scaled a vertical scaffolding, losing the two goons that were poorly following me.

Gavin didn't trust me, and rightfully so, but he was going to have to do better than that if he wanted to keep an eye on me.

Leaving their curses behind, I smirked as I landed on one of the adjacent alleyways. They might have been able to track me again, had I not quickly disappeared into a lingering fog of Malice that would be poisonous to untouched Dreg-dwellers. Luckily—or unluckily—I was definitely scarred by Malice enough to feel at home in even the thickest of Malice corruption.

Zizi landed on my shoulder and kicked her feet in that childlike manner that was so misleading. She was raw dark magic manifested from the Malice that had killed most of humanity, leaving those who remained segregated between the pompous fae-ruled lands of the Kingdom and the lawless outskirts known as the Dregs.

She grinned at me, her tiny fangs poking from plump lips—a fae trait. She could hear my thoughts when I didn't guard them from her. I didn't hide that I still distrusted her because of her origins. *You know you love me,* she teased.

I smirked and gently poked her in the ribs. "Only because you're cute."

She snapped her teeth, making me jerk away with mock-surprise. *I'm sexy and terrifying, not cute!*

She is, Steel chimed in.

I rolled my eyes. "You don't have to gang up on me."

I exited the fog of Malice only a few streets off course and glanced for any signs of Gavin's hired help. When no one tackled me to the ground, I decided that it was safe to proceed.

This isn't the way to the Kingdom, Zizi helpfully chided.

"We're making a detour."

The pixie huffed her annoyance. *Fine. When you're done wasting time, let me know.* She disappeared in a puff of smoke, leaving me feeling a fraction lighter than I had a moment before.

"Impatient pixie," I grumbled, although I knew the real reason she'd left.

The Breeder Nest had come into view.

The ancient building towered and almost rivaled the magnitude of the Northern Sector Guild with its grand stature and the purple aura that glowed behind it, moonlight hitting a wall of Malice that tangled against the protective barrier erected by the Malice Academy to keep such valuable establishments safe.

The Breeder Nest was more delicate in nature than the other structures of the Northern Sector and boasted an entire castle of female residents untouched by Malice. Even with its protective shield, the inevitable darkness of the Dregs tainted what had once been white walls with streaks of black marble. Ancient vines grew over the sides, blocking out windows and what might have been elegant statues. The glimpse of a feminine marble hand reaching through the foliage as if seeking for help always unnerved me.

Zizi had been the one to save me from the Breeder Nest, or so she claimed, but I think she still felt guilty for it. She said she came into existence the same time I did, both of us conceived in some dark room in this building. Since I was touched by Malice, I would have been useless to the Breeder Nest had my mother not sold me to the Casters. I shouldn't have lived through my childhood.

But you survived, Steel said, swimming around in my thoughts with silky invasion.

That I did.

A point I was proud of, even if I couldn't remember most of it.

I approached the tall, cracked doors and waited. The Breeder Mothers didn't like someone with Malice coming here, but I paid for my entry just like my father had. Enough crystals and anything could be bought in the Dregs… or the Kingdom.

My fingers fumbled against the new pouch in my cloak heavy with half of my payment for the job. Gavin had been right to send goons to watch over me because he knew I'd spend it before I even left the Dregs. I never held onto my crystals long, but I made a point to make sure he didn't find out where all my earnings went.

The door finally creaked open and a scowling headmistress greeted me.

Lady Helga.

She was beautiful, minus the slight crook of her nose where a patron had gotten too rough before she'd become headmistress. It'd never quite healed and jutted out to the side in a way that made her look like she was going to constantly sneeze. She glanced down at my hand that was still in my cloak and waited until I produced the pouch. I dumped out three crystals.

Light glowed from my hand, its radiance enough to compete with the shadows that licked around my fingers in an attempt to hide the treasure from any eyes that might be watching us. I frowned and released another gust of darkness around the entranceway, masking the exchange as best I could, but I'd never seen quality like this. Such exquisite crystals said that the fae were definitely involved with this job. Crap.

Lady Helga's eyes went wide and her lips took on a twisted quality that I guessed was a smile.

"That'll do," she whispered as I dropped the payment into her waiting hands.

She immediately shoved the treasure into her bodice that had enough layers to it to hide the glow as she glanced at my shadows. She wasn't afraid of Malice like most people. I guessed that she'd seen enough horror to know that Malice wasn't the worst thing in this world—not anymore, anyway. The damage had been done, humanity nearly wiped out and our new reality set in stone.

We lived and died by the whims of the fae, their neglect a result of creatures who'd brought Malice, leaving humanity to fend for ourselves on the outskirts of the last habitable land in our world.

"You're here to see Jilly, I presume?" she asked, getting to the point of my visit.

I gave her a curt nod. I often came to see Jilly, one of the girls on the cusp of maturity who reminded me of myself in some ways. In just a few short years she would be forced to take up her duties and I fully intended to get her out of here before that happened.

Even though my duties had been different, I wished that someone could have done the same for me.

I wondered what Lady Helga thought of my visits. She probably figured I was looking for an apprentice. It was difficult to infuse Malice into an adult, but possible. If anyone could do it safely, it would be me.

Jilly will never be touched by darkness of any kind, I vowed to myself. I couldn't save the world, but if I could save one innocent soul, then somehow every bad thing I'd done, every shadow I conjured, would at least have served a greater purpose.

Maybe it was too late for me, but it wasn't too late for Jilly.

Lady Helga swept through the dark corridors lit by the soft glow of fae crystals that betrayed the subtle wealth of the house. Most establishments used candles, but the Breeder Nest was well compensated. The healthy blues and golds from the less expensive crystals still outweighed what most would earn in an entire season through other guilds.

Guards that wedged themselves against the walls watched me as I followed the headmistress deeper into the Nest, their gazes calculating and skilled. More than a few played with inky wisps along their fingertips, likely having graduated from Malice Caster Academy and landed a coveted job at the Nest. Nothing was more valuable to the Dregs than crystals and untouched women, so it was even better guarded than the Northern Sector Guild itself, not that criminals needed many guards.

"She's just wrapping up her midnight exam," Lady Helga informed me as we reached one of the bedroom doors. She knocked twice as her lips twisted again. A second grin of the night from the headmistress? She was outright giddy.

Which meant I wasn't going to like what came next.

It took a few minutes for someone to open the door. When a pair of bushy brows and a familiar scowl stared down at me, I suddenly wasn't the most powerful Malice Caster in the Northern Sector Guild anymore, but a frightened child who knew nothing but the back of that man's hand and the sting of shadows that came with it.

Yorin, Headmaster of the Malice Caster Academy, was here.

My shadows stirred as my heart doubled its pace, adrenaline and the instinct to run pumping through my veins. Even Zizi poked her head out of the shadows just long enough to see what was going on and Steel's presence awakened in my mind. When Zizi spotted Yorin, she *yipped* like a kicked puppy and slipped back into the darkness again, Steel retreating along with her. Yorin was one of the few people who could actually see my Malice manifestations and he made a point to teach Zizi a lesson if she ever showed her face around him. He didn't care for puny Malice manifestations, as he called them.

"Penelope," he said, straightening and giving me a friendly nod as if we were on good terms.

Why did all the men who thought they owned me call me by that name?

"Penne," I corrected him, as was our usual exchange.

He gave me a slight nod, his midnight hair falling into his eyes. He was likely centuries old, but he was powerful in Malice and used it to keep himself young. His magically enhanced sharp jawline and too-bright eyes made him look eerie. Youth-keeping was a practice I disliked, given that the only way to build that kind of Malice for such powerful spells was to make others suffer, but there was no shortage of suffering when it came to Yorin.

Jilly's soft sobs accentuated my point and my fingers curled into fists, but I didn't shove past him like I wanted to. Instead, I waited and let my rage build. Suffering wasn't the only thing that could fuel Malice. Even though it wasn't as effective, my anger had saved me on more than one occasion.

"Lady Helga warned me you might try to stop us,

but you're too late. Jilly has been exposed to Malice and we'll know if she's a proper candidate for the Breeder Nest or... for the Academy."

Exposed.

She'd gotten through all fifteen years of her life without Malice infesting her soul. Now this bastard shoved it down her throat just to test if she could repel it—the most desirable talent needed by brood-mares of the Breeder Nest. It wasn't tested often, given the horrid success rate and loss of a perfectly good breeder.

Yorin rested a heavy hand on my shoulder and invaded my personal space, "Don't look so glum. Perhaps she'll join the Malice Academy. Won't that be fun?"

If she survives.

He waited, allowing the long, dramatic pause to make my instincts sing with the need to stab him in the eye. He tilted his head and gave me a smile that would have looked friendly on any other face. "I thought you'd be happy for her. If she takes to the Malice, she could join you at the Guild one day."

I couldn't suppress the growl that ripped through me. "You're a monster."

He chuckled, but there was an edge to his voice. Not many could talk to him that way, but I was

Gavin's dog now. He knew better than to risk ticking off the Guildmaster by killing me over a comment.

He drew back, his smile stitched on his face. "I'm a necessary evil in our world," he reminded me, then gave me a low nod. "I'll be on my way, if that's all right. My work here is done." He glanced at Lady Helga who frowned at our exchange, but she knew better than to interfere. "You'll let me know if she needs to be collected for the Academy, yes?" He flashed a new smile, this one genuine—which meant he highly suspected he was about to get a new student. That little relief was enough to let me breathe. Maybe Jilly would survive, which didn't necessarily mean she was Caster quality. "I'll pay the Breeder Nest handsomely for such a loss," he added.

"She's not yours yet," Lady Helga said, straightening and confident that she somehow had power over Malice when it came to her girls.

He bowed. "Of course. I will return in the morning." His shadows flickered, seeking me and I flinched away.

You'll never touch me or anyone I love ever again— one day, I'll have the power to stop you.

His shadows caressed my cheek with an invisible

kiss, like a father I never wanted who perverted the title.

And then he was gone.

Lady Helga opened her mouth to say something to me, but I shoved through the bedroom entrance and slammed the door in her face.

3

PENNE

"Jilly?" I asked, my voice gentle as I carefully approached the sobbing girl.

She shook and buried her face in her hands as she teetered back and forth on the edge of the bed. Malice clawed through her veins, showing on her skin with raised, raw, red and painful marks.

I swallowed the lump in my throat.

She definitely wasn't repelling the Malice, but she wasn't falling over dead, either. If she could get through the next twenty-four hours, she'd survive. If she showed any aptitude for the dark arts, she'd be signed up for Malice Caster Academy and be forced to live a criminal life she wasn't suited for.

"Jilly, I'm so sorry."

I should have been here sooner.

She finally lifted her tear-streaked face from her hands and sniffled at me. "Penne?" Her normally crisp blue eyes were cloudy with the heavy dose of Malice Yorin had given her.

I cursed. The bastard hadn't given her a chance. Even if she did possess the ability to repel Malice, no one could repel a dose like this without having *some* aptitude for its twisted magic. He wanted her for the Academy... or he wanted her dead.

But why?

With the amount of time he spent with the Seers, he no doubt saw what I had planned for Jilly tonight, but what I didn't get was why he cared.

Zizi appeared, startling me—and apparently Jilly. My friend jumped and covered her mouth on an open gasp. "What the Malice is that?"

I blinked. "You can see her?"

Of course she can see her, Steel huffed, as if that should be obvious, *the girl has enough Malice in her to put down a horse.*

I winced at the accurate assessment. In spite of Zizi's claims that she couldn't hear Steel's voice and denied he existed entirely, she flinched as well.

"It moved!" Jilly screeched, flailing back on the bed and reeling towards the wall.

"Zizi, you're scaring her," I said, which only made the dark pixie laugh.

She posed with both hands on her hips, flicking the shadows that made up her hair with pride. *What did I tell you? I'm terrifying.*

Rolling my eyes, I put myself between Zizi and Jilly. "Hey, it's all right. Remember I told I was talking to an annoying sprite sometimes? That's her, and apparently you can see her—for now, anyway."

What about me? Steel asked. I could almost hear him grinning.

"She doesn't need to know about you, too," I sneered in my lowest voice.

Jilly peered around my shoulder and her eyes went wide. "I always thought you were…"

"Knee-deep in crazy? Yeah, you and everyone else."

The familiar joke made Jilly relax. She gave me a weak smile. "Sorry, I guess it's just a bit overwhelming." She shifted her weight and then winced as shadows flickered through her system.

I sighed and kneeled on the bed, dropping my open palms onto my thighs. "I'm sorry, Jilly. This is my fault." Yorin didn't make a habit of personal visits to recruit new Casters. This had something to do with me.

Always thinking of others before herself, Jilly crawled over to me and grabbed both of my hands. I shivered at how cold she was, but I sensed the Malice in her body and what it was doing. It wasn't killing her—it was bonding with her.

No...

I had to stop it before it was too late.

Jilly squeezed my hands as if I was the one who needed comforting right now. "You're not going to blame yourself, you hear me? You're the only person in the Dregs who's ever given two cracked crystals about me. Stop looking so guilty." She forced a smile. "Did you bring me anything?"

Usually my visits coincided with a present or food. The Nesters were horribly underfed, supposedly to keep an "attractive" appearance. Jilly would have looked perfect with just a bit more meat on her so I brought her treats and fruit whenever I could.

Today, I brought something better.

One hand went to the splintered box strapped to my thigh. There was magic inside of it, and whatever it was, perhaps it would be enough to save Jilly.

But first, we had to get out of the Nest... and out of the Dregs entirely.

"We're leaving," I announced, having prepped Jilly as best as I could by conjuring her a black robe to wear. Her typical bright orange frilly dress definitely would stand out and we needed to blend in.

She stared at the open window. A few dead vines strangled the view, but for once, I was grateful for the ugly things. The gnarled plants would give Jilly enough purchase to climb down the three stories to the streets.

"I don't know if I can do this," she said, wringing her hands. Malice continued to streak through her skin as it buried itself under her fingernails. Her eyes, puffy from crying, now watched me with a sense of trepidation—but also trust. After all Jilly and I had been through over the years, I hoped that she knew by now I'd never let anything happen to her out on the streets.

I held out a hand and waited until she took it before drawing her closer to the window. Zizi fluttered at my shoulder, clearly making Jilly nervous. I glared at the pixie. "Why don't you make yourself useful and go keep watch?"

Zizi gave an unladylike snort and pinched my cheek. Her icy fingers did little to affect me and her nip felt more like a small breeze to a Malice Caster like me. *Fine, but for the record, I told you this was a bad idea.*

Of course it was a bad idea. If we were caught, Jilly would be put in an air-tight prison—otherwise known as a classroom in Malice Academy—and I would be tortured until Gavin was satisfied that I'd learned my lesson. No one stole from the Breeder Nest and lived to talk about it, at least, not without a few scars added to their back.

Jilly knew the risks, but she squeezed my hand anyway and lifted one leg over the windowsill. Lady Helga could have put us in a room without windows, but she underestimated my fear of Northern Sector reprimand. It's not a mistake she would make twice, so I'd better get this right the first time.

"Up you go," I said and lifted Jilly the rest of the way. She gripped onto the vines and grimaced.

"They have thorns," she complained.

Of course they do. Stupid Malice.

There wasn't much I could do about that, but I sent enough shadows cooling at her fingertips that it would numb the pain.

She glanced at me when my shadows gave a low shriek of protest. "You should let me feel it," she offered. "It'll feed your Malice."

She was right.

Suffering.

The amount of emotional distress she was in already gave my Malice an edge. The pain from the thorns she experienced could feed my magic and make it stronger, but I had more than enough for today's job. "It's all right," I assured her as I climbed over the edge and began my descent. "I'll have to bind my Malice where we're going, anyway."

She gave me a wide-eyed stare before turning her attention back to the thorns, setting her footing with her delicate flats before attempting another step down.

You're going to WHAT? Zizi screeched, making Jilly stumble.

Yeah, I didn't agree to this, Steel added in my head.

I swatted at the pixie and she zipped around me with aggressive maneuvers. "We'll talk about it when we're safe... on the *ground*," I growled and sent a wave of Malice over the pixie that held her at bay. I had practiced binding my powers before, even though Zizi thought I was insane. It would be a necessary measure in the Kingdom where fae could sniff out Malice like well-trained dogs.

I filled myself with resolve while Jilly and I made slow work of our downward climb. I could have descended in two seconds flat, but I kept one foot below Jilly, ready to catch her if she fell. Perhaps I was too much in my thoughts, or anxious about getting Jilly to safety, but my guard was down.

I noticed the invading cold too late.

My Malice always came over me like ice, a cold so frigid it could feel hot sometimes... but another sort of wave settled over me and secured itself around my ankles until it'd gotten a firm hold—and then it yanked.

An involuntary screech came from my mouth as I catapulted off the vine wall and was tossed to the ground like a rag doll. I bounced when I hit the unforgiving streets, taking the brunt of the force on my left side and a crack resonated through my body. Pain exploded behind my eyelids and my Malice lapped it up with greedy hunger. There could never be enough pain or suffering for the dark fog that had linked itself to my heart.

That surge of power was enough to sweep a healing wave that sealed my broken rib back into place. My instincts kicked in, putting up a shield for the blow that came next.

Two Malice Casters sent a tumult of Malice beating down on me that *pinged* hard against my barrier.

I should have known that Lady Helga wouldn't

have been so naive. She'd been headmistress of the Breeder's Nest long enough to know how to keep her girls in line. She crossed her arms as she glowered at me from a safe distance behind the two attackers.

I recognized the Casters from the Academy. Ron and Jayce took turns sending inky black spears of magic at my shield, beating me down until my knee ground into the unforgiving street.

"Stop it!" Jilly screeched as Zizi helped her out of the Malice net she'd conjured to catch my best friend. I was relieved that my pixie was there for me when it mattered.

"Aw, what's the problem?" Jayce sneered, flicking his midnight hair from his face, "You don't want me to make an example of this little lost sheep?" He thought he was so clever and so handsome. I wanted to break his nose so he could match Lady Helga.

Ron crossed his arms and smirked, nudging closer to the Malice Caster. "Told you she'd survive the fall." His dark eyes twinkled at me. He'd always had a thing for me and loved to test me. Whenever I survived the latest attack, he boasted how I'd be his mate one day.

In your nightmares, Caster boy.

Jayce readied another spear. "I missed the first time. Let's see if she can block this one."

"Enough," Lady Helga snapped, unamused by the pair. She hated Casters, but she loved their crystals. "Yorin said that Penelope is to remain unharmed. Your job is to keep Jilly in the Nest until her twenty-four hour period is up, understand?" She pointed a finger almost as crooked as her nose at the castle. "Now focus on the task."

Grumbling, the pair approached a crumpled Jilly still recovering from her tumble to the ground, even if it was broken by Zizi's net. She shook it off and balled her fists and shot to her feet, ready to fight.

That's my girl, I thought.

I didn't have enough Malice to take on two top-class Casters like Ron and Jayce, especially after the pummeling they'd given my shield. I'd been preparing to bind my powers... not set them loose, and Malice sputtered at my fingertips, only intact because of the pain throbbing from my broken rib that wouldn't fully heal without more Malice.

Zizi bobbed up and down, anxiously trying to put herself between Jilly and the two Casters, but they swatted her aside as if she was nothing and her tiny screech of pain sent me over the edge.

Aren't you forgetting a little something you brought along with you? Steel asked.

I glanced down at the box secured to my hip which had helped to break my fall. A crack down the middle revealed something gold and luminous inside…

Something fae.

I didn't have time to question the sanity of sticking my hand in the box, so I did it without thinking and wrapped my fingers around the warm metal that hummed with foreign power. Power that was so opposite of my Malice that I gasped when raw heat and sunlight flooded into my body, burning the dark cold as if it were a plague.

Light shot from my body and the Casters jerked to a halt, turning only long enough to see the blast coming straight for them. They covered their eyes against the blinding heat, Lady Helga adding her own screech to the mix. The blast effortlessly knocked them aside, leaving Jilly gaping at me with darkness swirling in her eyes.

Running to her, I grabbed her by the wrist and she shrieked in pain as the sunlight funneled through me and into her. I felt what it was doing—it was destroying any Malice it touched—and I couldn't allow it to change me completely. I guarded the cold encasement of Malice that scarred my heart like a bad memory. It was a part of me and without it, I knew I wouldn't survive.

But Jilly could.

Her Malice was still new, unseated. Sunlight tore through her and blistered in her veins, scalding away the sickness with unforgiving heat.

Pain like I'd never experienced ricocheted back to me through our connection, but I didn't let go. I allowed her pain to fuel my Malice, giving me the foothold I needed to be a conduit of both darkness and light. "Hang on!" I yelled over the roar of magic that pummeled the air.

In a brilliant flash, it was done, and Jilly's eyes rolled in the back of her head as she fell. I caught her and ran.

I didn't look back.

4

PENNE

I knew that I looked like a madwoman running through the Dregs holding an unconscious Jilly whose cloak was hopelessly ruined. Her dress, though, gleamed with golden sequins and she would fit in where we were going.

I approached the checkpoint with my heart in my throat and a scowling guard stepping out to block my path.

"What's the meaning of this?" he barked, glancing at Jilly and then back at me.

I knew what it looked like. The light had changed Jilly, given her skin a permanent glow that said there was only one place she belonged now.

She was an Elite—and I was a ruffian carrying her limp form like a kidnapping gone wrong.

"I'm returning this citizen to the Kingdom," I said, my voice firm as I pressed Jilly tightly to my chest. Malice and adrenaline coursed through me and gave me the strength to hold her without breaking a sweat. Even if she was tiny, I'd just run through the entire Northern Sector with her in my arms. Not exactly the covert mission I was going for, but sometimes I had to go with the flow.

He's not going to let you in looking like that, Zizi chided, fluttering out of a sputtering of Malice that had somehow survived the onslaught of power.

Zizi formed the Malice with skilled strokes, forming a small mirror that showed blonde curls escaped from my cowl and Malice that no longer clouded my eyes, revealing the sharp blue of what they would have been—had I been human.

Beautiful, even without shadows, Steel said, his words sliding over me like velvet.

Always the charmer.

Working the change in my favor, I continued the process to bind my Malice into the tiny core in my heart. Whatever the artifact was in the box that I'd drawn from, it was powerful and it had already started the process of binding the Malice within me. The Light would have destroyed my Malice completely had I not had Jilly for an outlet.

"I'm her guardian," I snapped when the man's hand went to the weapon at his belt. I had a pathetic dagger strapped to my thigh, but I'd need more than a short blade to get past this ogre. The entrance guards to the Kingdom were given fae weapons and I did not want that curved blade coming at my face.

"How do I know you're not just looking for ransom?" he retorted.

His buddy, a larger man who'd been watching the exchange from his post, sauntered over and crossed his arms. "If you're really her guardian, then you'll have a badge," he added, then grinned, revealing cracked, yellow teeth, "or enough crystals to make us say you had a badge."

And there it was, the root of all Malice in the world. It fed off of pain and suffering, but that pain and suffering was a result of corruption and greed.

I knew that, but it still turned my stomach and I frowned, shifting Jilly to reach for the pouch of crystals that luckily had remained inside my coat pocket. I pulled it out and held the drawstring with my teeth, opening the bag enough to see how many crystals I had left.

The guard didn't give me a chance to pull out an adequate payment for illegal entry into the Kingdom and snatched the entire thing from my grasp. If I hadn't had an unconscious Jilly in my grasp, I would have taught him a lesson.

Instead, I waited.

He weighed the bag in his palm and gave me a twisted grin. "Hmm, I don't know, it feels heavy enough to be a badge, what do you think?" he asked his friend and offered the pouch.

I wrapped what Malice was left around myself as the guard frowned, looking as if he was going to be one of the few who might not be bribed, but then he glanced at Jilly and a flash of empathy crossed his face. "It's a badge. Let her through."

I cursed under my breath, because I'd been stupid enough not to save some crystals in another pouch. That was all the advance Gavin had given me.

Rookie mistake.

You're off your game today, Zizi helpfully offered. *That's what you get for binding the* best *part of you.*

I opened my mouth to tell her off, but then closed it again as guilt wafted over me. She faded, her entire body going translucent and the onyx gems she wore like a crown twinkling out of existence at her head. She sighed. *I'll still be here, okay? But I can't keep a corporeal form without your Malice roaming free.*

I'll be gone too, Steel said, sounding uncharacteristically forlorn, *but I'll be waiting for your return.*

I gave a stiff nod. Zizi and I had a love-hate relationship, but it still gave me mixed feelings to watch her begin to vanish before my eyes. Steel's periodic comments, however, I felt like I could learn to live without.

Zizi smiled before disappearing completely in a puff of smoke. Her voice trickled into my mind.

You're never alone. I promise.

With that last bit of reassurance, I shoved past the guards and bound the last of my Malice in my heart. Everything about the air changed when I crossed the border that wound its long golden line between the Dregs and the Kingdom. Something lifted, as if I'd been swimming in a fog all my life. A new sensation swept over me as the sweet scent of peaches and apples tinged my nose. A soft melody drifted in the background as if coming from nowhere and everywhere.

Jilly's eyelids fluttered, her body reacting to the lift of Malice that she could no longer handle.

"Don't worry," I whispered as I began down a golden street illuminated by moonlight, "you'll never have to live in a nightmare again."

Without opening her eyes, she smiled.

Fae... I hoped I wasn't lying to her.

I'D BEEN to the Kingdom only a handful of times before. Gavin had clients all over, including a few Elites. Never fae, though, and I wondered again who that stranger was that had such a powerful artifact— much less who would have been stupid enough to hand it over to a man like Gavin.

And why the flipping fae had the stranger wanted the artifact to be sent to Malice Caster Academy? That was the most confusing thing of all. Malice Casters would have studied it, learned how the fae controlled them and kept Malice out of the Kingdom. It could have destroyed everything.

Or is there something you're missing? Zizi's voice offered.

I frowned. "Pretty sure Malice and Fae Magic don't go together," I grumbled at her, feeling unnerved that I could hear her in my head but she couldn't flit around me in her pixie form anymore. "Are you... all right?" I asked her. When I'd bound my Malice before, it had never felt this... permanent, and Zizi had never lost her body.

I'll be fine, she promised. *It's kind of exciting, actually. I can see everything you can see.*

I sighed. "Great, that's not creepy or stalkerish at all."

She giggled, then she yawned. *I don't have to be here all the time. In fact, a nap sounds nice.* Her voice faded and my sense of her diminished as if her consciousness recessed into the back of my mind.

Could she go... dormant?

This was getting too weird.

Jilly stirred in my arms and I carefully lowered her to the ground. She clung to me and blinked a few times. "Where are we? What happened?" she asked, then touched her throat and looked at me with concern widening her gaze.

Yeah, I'd heard it too, that faint tinkling in the way she spoke that I'd only heard from Elites.

I grinned at her. "Your life is about to change, that's what happened," I said with a chuckle, relief flooding through me because it looked like she was going to be all right. Then dread crept in as I remembered that I had no crystals left, nothing to pay her way into an Academy House.

Jilly glanced down at my robe that obscured the artifact. It called to her, just as it was still calling to me. It hadn't finished what it'd started, although it'd accomplished a lot in its short explosion of release. "What is that thing?" she asked.

My hand went to the side of the box. Hmm, maybe if I didn't have crystals, this could be my payment. "It's your ticket to a new life, come on," I said and grabbed her hand, new resolve launching me into a speed walk down the street.

She stumbled to keep up, her flats having transformed into golden sequined adornments that clinked with her steps. "Holy fae, where are we?"

The Kingdom was impressive, even at night, or maybe especially so. The city was out of old human fairytales, complete with a white castle at the center. Butterflies loped around trimmed grassy fields that spanned the large expanse between us and the Crown Princess Academy, a place I hoped I or Jilly would never have to experience for ourselves.

Poor bastards who were dragged into its walls...

I couldn't save everyone, no matter how much I tried. Right now my job was to get Jilly to a place where she would have shelter, allies, and a chance at a decent life among the Elites.

"We're in the Kingdom and I'm taking you to the Rose Academy House," I told her. She jerked my hand, making me halt.

"Academy House?" she shrieked. "Look, Penne, I know you're trying to help, but after everything you've told me about the Kingdom's Academy, it's even worse than the Malice Casters."

While true, there wasn't much choice in the matter. Which was why I was going to take her to the Academy House with the worst candidate record. "You're not actually going to go to the Academy, okay? The Rose Academy House raises girls from Elite families, but they have a ten percent success rate. There's no way you'll be chosen as a Princess Candidate, yet the Elites respect the Houses. You're fifteen, which means you only have to stay there for three years before you can choose your own life. It'll open up opportunities for you." Her wide eyes filled with apprehension and fear and made my heart twist. I squeezed her hand. "Look, it's the best I can do for you, okay? Do you really want to go back?"

She glanced behind us at the patch of darkness on the horizon—the Dregs. Inky blackness spanned in a long loop around the Kingdom, boxing it in and making me feel trapped. Funny, I'd never felt like that when I was inside of the blackness, unable to look out at the world around us.

"I never want to go back," Jilly said, straightening with resolve. She set her jaw and gave me a firm nod. "So, Academy House. Okay, I can do that."

She took my hand again and we walked together down the golden streets, ignoring the few servants who passed nervous glances our way.

"Maybe you should take off the cloak," I offered. There wasn't much left of it anyway, and it hung loosely around her shoulders like a shadow.

She shrugged it off and let the ratty fabric fall to the ground as we continued walking. She was breathtaking, her golden dress now fitting perfectly to once girlish curves that seemed to have enhanced into a more womanlier figure after her exposure to the fae magic I'd released. She definitely looked the part of an Elite. She swiped her hand over her face as I stared at her. "I look ridiculous, don't I?"

Chuckling, I squeezed her hand as I pulled aside my cowl, allowing my blonde curls the rare chance to unfurl over my shoulders. "This make you feel any better?"

She smirked. "I've never met another Malice Caster with blonde hair like yours. Are you sure you're not part fae?"

"Don't even joke about that," I chuckled and took a turn onto one of the narrow streets that wound around the edge of the fields. "We're almost there."

A few of my trips to the Kingdom had revolved around the Rose Academy House. Given their low success rate of their girls being chosen as candidates for the Crown Princess Academy, they had to do something to stay in business. Gavin had fae connections better than some Elites and, in exchange for crystals, would put in a good word for the Academy. I still found it hard to believe that Gavin once was an Elite himself before being exposed to Malice.

The reminder of how much the Kingdom hated Malice made me clamp down on that cold bottled inside my chest just a fraction more.

Not so hard, Zizi's voice complained, her words slurred as if I'd woken her up.

"Sorry," I muttered.

Jilly gave me a raised brow. "You don't have to apologize. You got me out of the Dregs."

I chuckled. "We're not out of the woods yet."

We approached a mansion with roses primped along its border until the entire perimeter overflowed with reds, pinks, and blues. Jilly's eyes widened. "Let me guess, this is the Rose Academy House?"

I nodded and let go of her hand, trusting her to follow me. "Yep, now let me do the talking." I hadn't quite worked out how I was going to convince the headmistress to take Jilly on, but the one thing Elites liked more than their pretty properties was fae magic, and I happened to have a box full of it.

Marching up the wide, marble steps, I paused before the looming mahogany doors and tugged on the heavy metal knocker, letting it fall twice to thrum a magical boom throughout the foyer.

When the door didn't open, I motioned for Jilly to stand next to me. "They'll open it if they can see you."

She gathered her dress and clinked on over to my side, smoothing the glimmering rolls of fabric. "What did you do to my dress, anyway?" she asked under her breath.

Before I could respond, the door cracked open and a butler stared us down. He swept his gaze over me and scowled, but he didn't shout the alarm. Very few Dreg-dwellers had blonde hair anymore and it was the one thing that helped me fit in during my trips to the Kingdom.

When his gaze landed on Jilly, he smiled. "Ah, you must be a new lady for the House, I presume?"

Yes, I thought, hoping he'd take the bait, *Jilly's going to be a Lady.*

Jilly gave a curtsey that had me gaping. I couldn't have played the role better myself. "I'm sorry for the late hour, sir, but we have a perfectly good explanation, if we could see the headmistress?"

He glanced at me again before chewing his lip, then nodded. "Yes, yes. Can't have you standing on our doorstep on the Eve of the Selection, now can we?" He ushered us into a glamorous foyer complete with glimmering fae crystal chandeliers and roses blooming from the walls. The flora sent bursts of sickening sweetness into the air and I wrinkled my nose.

"She'll be right down," he added with a sweeping gesture. "Please make yourselves comfortable," the butler offered, motioning to the lounge chairs. "I'm to apologize for the lack of tea at this hour."

I glanced at the empty silver platters that still boasted a few stale biscuits. The butler moved to clean it up. "It's all right," I told him with a smile, hoping he couldn't hear my stomach grumble with excitement, "we'd like to see the headmistress immediately, if that's acceptable. As you said, it's the eve of the Selection." Whatever the flipping fae that meant.

He nodded and bowed before scurrying up the long spiral of steps. Apparently the Selection was a big deal.

When he'd disappeared, I gathered the fistful of crackers and offered them to Jilly. "Hungry?"

She smirked. "You seem far more ravenous than I. Help yourself."

Shrugging, I shoved the treats into my mouth and then groaned as the delicacies melted on my tongue. "Oh, you're missing out," I said around the mouthful.

Jilly giggled as I devoured the rest of the crackers, forcing a few on her, then went searching if there were any other abandoned trays.

Just when I'd found one biscuit that had slipped between a tray and an adjacent table, a woman cleared her voice. I glanced up to meet the gaze of one of the more attractive Elites I'd had the pleasure of working with on occasion. Luckily, I'd always been doused in shadows and my trusty cowl, so she didn't recognize me now.

The headmistress was a tall woman with a firm stance, but with soft features that still made her approachable. Her hair, a stark red, flowed over her shoulders in waves that were reminiscent of a rose.

"Lady Rose, I presume," I said, smiling and brushing away crumbs. "Thank you for seeing us. You might not know me. I'm—"

"Penelope of the Criminal Sector Guild and Malice Caster," she said with a scowl, as if my name left a sour taste in her mouth.

Oh. Apparently she did recognize me.

She glanced at Jilly who'd gone ramrod straight. "And you, I suppose, are Jilly of the Breeder Nest and soon to be property of Malice Academy." She tilted her head, her gaze sweeping over Jilly's golden gown and enhanced features. "Although, you don't really look the part. Perhaps Gavin made a mistake with his message."

I cursed under my breath. Of course Gavin would have had his feelers out for whatever I'd been up to, especially anything that involved Malice Academy. I hadn't expected him to betray me to the Elites, though.

This only meant one thing.

I couldn't return to the Dregs—not without a fight.

Focusing on the task at hand, I shoved aside my own concerns for what the fae I was going to do now and unraveled what was left of the ropes that strapped the artifact's box to my hip. Light filtered out into the foyer and Lady Rose's eyes went wide.

"How about a trade? Fae magic in exchange for taking on my friend as a Lady of the House." I stuck up one finger. "But she won't be chosen as a candidate for Crown Princess Academy." That would possibly be even a worse fate than Jilly being forced into Malice Academy.

Lady Rose's gaze didn't leave the box in my hands. "Dear fae," she said on an expelled breath as she slowly approached, her long gown swishing between her thighs. "Do you even realize what you hold, my dear?"

Lady Rose approached and rested her hands on either side of the box, seeming careless of any splinters she might get from its sharp edges, and tugged it apart as if she were peeling an orange.

Light billowed out into the room and then, for the first time, I realized what I had in my possession, and why I was even more doomed than I had realized.

A tiny crown—a mark of one chosen to be a Crown Princess Initiate... and I had activated it and used its power.

Zizi stirred from the depths of my mind.

Well, I'll be a Light Fae, she murmured, *looks like you're going to the Academy in Jilly's place.*

5

LUCAS

*T*he crown was *supposed* to go to Malice Caster Academy. It was *supposed* to be destroyed, creating a cascade effect that would have brought the whole system down.

Yet I sensed that the crown had chosen a candidate.

In the *Dregs?*

Flipping Fae.

The plan should have been simple. Malice Casters had Malice. Malice destroyed Light. Therefore, the crown should have been destroyed, taking with it the other crowns that governed entrance to Crown Princess Academy. Instead, it did exactly what it was designed to do: find a candidate and give her power over Light… never mind that she was a Malice Caster.

It shouldn't have worked. It didn't make sense. Elites trained their entire lives to qualify for Crown Princess Academy. How could one touched by Malice so easily find her way into the Queen's Class? This was unsettling proof that both Light and Malice could be mixed.

What did that mean?

Nothing good, that's for sure.

"Ah, do you feel that, my son?" my father, the Fae Crowned King purred as he swept his hands over a long row of tiny duplicate crowns that glowed to life. They represented the crowns that had been sent out across the Kingdom to bring another round of potential princesses to the Academy. "Another candidate has been chosen." He beamed with pride. "Soon, I will return to the Fae Realm and you will take your rightful place as Crown King." His smile dimmed when he perused the crowns again. "Although it's odd that there are seven crowns. I thought we had only sent out six crowns, I must be getting senile in my old age."

"Oh?" I asked, trying to sound bored, although my heart had just jumped in my throat. When I'd stolen the crown for the Northern Sector, I hadn't expected a candidate to be chosen.

Don't look guilty. Don't look him in the eye. Keep calm.

My father glanced at me, sending all the blood draining from my face.

I'm so dead.

The king stroked his chin. "Do you know anything of this?"

I shrugged. "Perhaps you miscounted, Father." I cleared my throat as beads of sweat formed at my hairline. When in doubt of how to proceed, go with flattery. "Regardless, I'm impressed. You must have done your job ruling the Kingdom for the crowns to find so many worthy initiates."

He hummed his agreement, seeming pleased with the praise. "Perhaps." He grinned. "Just as you will when your turn to rule comes."

I adjusted the band of light strapped around my forehead that marked me as the Crown Prince. There would be no more kings if I had my way.

I am not like them. The fae don't deserve humanity— don't deserve me.

There had to be a way to bring the system down and I was going to find it.

The fae who was my father was just as much a stranger to me as the rest of the Elites in the Kingdom. After my birth, I'd been sent to the Fae Realm while my mother ruled by the Crown King's side, but she didn't leave me with nothing. She planted her guiding voice, hopes and dreams in my mind. The fae had never been able to brainwash me thanks to her foresight.

It'd killed her to give me that magical, moral compass and I wrapped my fingers over the rail, vowing to get revenge. My own father, my people, they had taken her from me and were going to do it again to some other poor soul.

My father was so proud, as if he wasn't responsible for the death of my mother. He motioned to the expanse of the Kingdom that spread out beneath the balcony. He'd ruled for nineteen years and he thought that he was actually doing humanity a service.

"Your future bride is out there, somewhere. The crowns have selected worthy candidates and they are ready to be plucked like the ripe fruit that they are." His eyes glimmered. "Are you anxious to meet them tomorrow?"

A bunch of sniveling Elite females who voluntarily were walking to their deaths? It baffled me that they were really naive enough to think they'd survive the Queen's Class.

Malice, no, I wasn't anxious. I was revolted by the idea of playing my part in this sick charade.

In an effort to hide my reaction, I rested my forearms over the railing and pretended to look over my future domain. I glowered at the view, internally vowing that the fae—and my father—would get what they deserved.

"I'm sure the candidates are much more anxious than I," I offered after a moment's silence. "Not all of them will survive, after all," I reminded him.

The Queen's Class was a game of life and death. That's how a Queen was really chosen. She not only had to look the part, but she had to withstand the onslaught of fae magic that would be thrown at her, as well as the final test. Even though a number of graduates from Crown Princess Academy would be given lofty roles in Fae society, the Queen's Class would not be so lenient.

Only one candidate would come out of this alive.

The king nodded, joining me to gaze at the golden and whitewashed city. Its spires formed a barrier against the blackened backdrop of Malice that had nearly devoured this entire world. "Most won't *graduate*," he corrected, sugarcoating the truth.

I clamped my jaw to keep from blurting out a

retort. Thanks to my mother's teachings, I didn't view humans as things to be used and discarded. Just because fae-kind had lost the ability to breed those with magic didn't mean I approved of how human females were selected as surrogates. With enough Light, even a human could breed with the fae and produce offspring that would continue our race's magic.

Even if there was a cost.

There was always a cost.

My mother made sure I knew that humanity had so much more potential than breeding. Malice twisted them if not properly guided, and the fae certainly weren't helping matters by encouraging the segregation between the Dregs and the Kingdom. Given more time, humans could have become a powerful force even greater than the fae. Instead, we'd stunted their growth to use them for our own gain. It sickened me.

What pained me most was that I couldn't hear my mother's voice anymore. I'd never even seen her face, but I felt as if I could close my eyes and she would be there. That's how strong her magic was. But that was also before my return to the Kingdom and my placement at the Academy. My magic strained here among so much Malice. I refused to let her go, even if her magic in me waned. The effort to hold onto her left me feeling more angry and alone than I'd ever been in all my life.

"I know the Candidates are anxious to meet you," my father pressed. "One of them will become your Queen and she will be given all the power the fae have to offer."

Yes, such a blessing to be dosed with so much magic that it would tear a human apart over the course of a few short years, just like it had done to my mother. "Don't you grow bored of it?" I asked, unable to help myself. I had to know if there was any remorse in him at all.

He gave me a raised brow. "Bored of what?"

I kept my gaze locked on the murky horizon. "Every nineteen years a new fae takes his place as Crown King over the human world, but there's not much of a Kingdom to rule." I motioned to the inky blackness that closed in around the Kingdom. "Malice only grows stronger, not weaker. We're not making any progress."

He chuckled, the sound a low rumble that made my skin prickle. "I suppose the truth has been hidden from you for long enough." I dared a glance at him over my shoulder and his lips tightened. "You might not have agreed to take the crown if you'd known that Malice can never be defeated. It is indeed a losing battle."

As if I had a choice.

"Then why are we here?"

The King sighed. "It's time you know the full truth, my son."

Truth? I'm all ears, I thought, gripping the balcony's rail until my fingers went numb.

"The Dark Fae want nothing more than to destroy life," my father began, dashing my hopes that he might tell me something of value. Of course, the Dark Fae were to blame for everything. The perfect scapegoat. "If not for quick action among our Elites, all could have been lost during the first wave of Malice all those years ago. As you know, the Dark Fae conjured Malice, rendering newborn Fae to be born without magic or immortality. What you do not know is that Malice contaminated our power— our Light—and continues to threaten our world."

I raised an eyebrow. He wanted to play this game? All right. I knew that Malice had taken the Light from my people, it's why I was here. I was a rarity among the fae now. Only the Crown Prince and Crown King had the old gifts anymore. I liked to think that's why I was different, but my father continued to disappoint me. "Are you telling me that

Malice can do worse than take away a fae's light? What do you mean by 'contaminate?'"

My father frowned. "The Dark Fae aren't a separate race, my son. They were once creatures of Light. They were once one of *us*."

I stilled. That didn't surprise me, given the corruption already in fae hearts, but I put on a show of acting appalled by the idea. "Is that so? How troubling."

"Indeed," he said with a nod. "Without the Academy, they could add to their own number, and spread pestilence and death to those who don't conform." His eyes sparkled with determination. "The Human Realm is all that stands between us and them. It is our duty to keep this hub of humanity intact, the final barrier between the Dark Fae and our home. We can't waste our resources trying to expand the Kingdom. Maintaining the line of defense, as well as having a son of your own, will be your duty." He clapped me on the back, making me tense. "You'll do a fine job. Don't look so depressed." A grin as dark as Malice stretched across his face. "And when you have your Queen, you'll understand the reward that comes with your sacrifice."

A flicker of inky blackness swept across his eyes. Power forbidden to the Light Fae, too chaotic and uncontrolled to be handled without going insane. Or perhaps… that was exactly how a fae turned Dark.

Malice.

I shoved him away. "I thought you said that Malice is what poses a threat to our people, yet you embrace it? Do you wish to become a Dark Fae?"

He swept his fingers through silver hair. He was twice my age, which wasn't much by fae standards, but life in the Kingdom had aged him. "That, my son, is the sacrifice. I'll die before I turn, but it could be centuries before that might happen." He tapped his chest. "I have a safeguard in place. If I am completely depleted of Light, my heart will stop and prevent me from becoming a threat to our people." He smirked at my dropped jaw. This time, I was genuinely surprised. "When you become King, you will take this burden from me. It is why we are here. Light magic can no longer produce life, but humans provide us with a loophole. The right Queen will be able to survive the bonding and the next Crown King will be born." He rested a heavy hand on my shoulder and I resisted the urge to fling him off again. "Until we deal with the Dark Fae, this is how it must be done. Do you understand?"

He waited until I gave him a nod before he backed off.

He adjusted the cuffs at his wrists, his tell that he knew I was ticked off. If he expected me to fall to his feet at this great revelation, he had another thing coming. He wanted me to tell him that I would do anything to keep the royal line going, even if it meant embracing Malice so that I might have an heir.

I hated Malice almost as much as I hated him.

My father cleared his throat. "The guard will accompany you to collect the Candidates in the morning," he said, then put on his fake smile again. "You'll warm up to the idea once you meet so many capable women vying to rule at your side. Trust me."

Oh, trust is the last thing you'll get from me... Father.

6

PENNE

"Are you kidding me?" I shrieked, spinning halfway in a circle only for my very *pink* and *fluffy* dress to follow my movements in a flash of sparkle and fae magic. A kiss of steel hugged my leg, so at least my dagger was still intact, but the rest of me was all too fru fru to handle.

"I think it's pretty," Jilly offered with a giddy smile. "And that crown… Oh, Penne, you look just adorable."

Tentatively I reached up to feel the blasted thing on my head. "This is *ridiculous!*" Glowering at Lady Rose, I decided that I didn't care if she called half the Kingdom guard down on me; I wasn't going to let this happen. "Take it off me!"

Lady Rose blinked, her red hair gracefully draped

over her heaving chest as she tried to gulp in breaths of air. "My dear, you've been chosen by the crown as a candidate." She waved out her hands with disbelief. "You… are to attend Crown Princess Academy." She leaned in, examining the crown. "It seems as one of the Queen's Class, no less."

I cursed again under my breath and reached for the Malice in my heart, but the transformation from the crown had sealed it away tighter than I ever could have done on my own. Even Zizi's voice seemed lost to me, her slumbering shadow somewhere so deep in my consciousness that I worried I'd never be able to get her out again.

"Blasted Fae!" I shouted, making Lady Rose blush at my foul mouth. She scanned the room as if a hundred fae would pop out of nowhere and slay us all for the insult.

"I have a deal for you to consider," Lady Rose said, her eyes glimmering with delight. She took Jilly's hand and squeezed. "I'll accept your friend, but on one condition. That you pronounce yourself as a member of Rose Academy House when the Fae Crown Guard come to collect you in the morning."

"Oh no," I said, waving my hands, "I'm not staying here. I'm not going to be anywhere in the vicinity for anybody to come 'collect' me, nope. And I'm certainly not going to the Academy."

Jilly's eyes pleaded with me. "Penne, I've never seen you like this," she said, her laughter diminishing into genuine concern. "I know you said the Academy was bad, but if you can't handle it, then what hope is there for any of the other girls?"

"*Handle* it?" Lady Rose huffed. "There is no greater honor in all of Elite society. Why in the seven realms would you turn down candidacy for Crown Princess Academy? Your initiation alone— with our name attached—will bring us enough clients to keep this House more than comfortably funded until the next Queen's Class Selection."

I glowered at the brainwashed woman. I knew there was nothing I could say or do to convince her of the truth, but one glance back at Jilly's worried face told me that I didn't have a choice. She would be safe here and just because I'd gone and screwed up didn't mean she had to pay the price.

"Fine," I said, curling my fingers into the fabric that puffed around my thighs. "I'll do it, but if anything, and I mean *anything* happens to Jilly, I will tell them everything and this House will be shut down for good."

Lady Rose gave a firm nod. "You have my word

Jilly will be in good hands." As if to demonstrate that quite literally, she patted Jilly's face and wrapped an arm around her shoulder. "I'll show you to your quarters, dear." She smiled at me. "You too, Penelope. You must get your rest before your big day tomorrow."

Right, because every princess needs her beauty sleep.

This is going to suck.

———

LADY ROSE DIDN'T LIKE it when I insisted that Jilly and I stay in the same room, but I had a nagging feeling this would be the last time I'd ever see my friend. I needed to say goodbye.

I sucked at goodbyes.

"Do you think you'll meet the King?" Jilly asked, her eyes having an uncharacteristic sparkle to them as she teetered on the edge of the bed.

The silver nightgown fit her like a glove and her transformation still amazed me. Jilly had always been pretty, but now she was absolutely stunning. Fae magic changed her and I chewed on my lower lip, worried that the change had been more than just skin-deep.

69

I touched the crown still on my head. It refused to be removed and I hoped I wouldn't have to sleep with it every night I was in the Academy. "I'm sure the King will be there. I mean, that's where he lives."

She giggled and kicked her feet. I hadn't seen her this giddy, well, ever. "And the Crown Prince will be there too! Fae... What if you graduate? What if *you* become the Crown Princess and inherit the Kingdom as Queen?" Her eyes sparkled at the idea. "Think of all the good you could do."

I frowned. "Queen Penne. Yeah, doesn't have a ring to it."

She waved a hand at me. "You have to go by Penelope now, of course. Just like I'll have to be called Julianna."

I wrinkled my nose. "Jilly fits you better."

She shrugged and patted the empty space next to her. "If using my formal name is the sacrifice I must make in order to stay out of the Dregs, it's a small sacrifice indeed."

Relenting, I shrugged off the last of my pink fluffy dress and put on a nightgown. The dress glimmered on the chair and tugged at me to put it back on again. I poked at my crown. "I already have to sleep with you on my head. I am *not* sleeping in that dress, too."

A chill ran down my spine, then the compulsion to put on the puffy pink mess subsided.

Jilly—Julianna gave me a raised brow. "Is the crown talking to you?"

"Not talking," I said. "Persuasion."

Compulsion magic wasn't a novel concept, although it was rare. Malice Casters needed a lot of power to bend someone to their will. They often just chose the route of fearmongering and torture. Much faster.

Jilly offered me a raised brow, her gaze flicking up to the crown again. "It has a lot of magic, doesn't it?"

I sighed. "Yeah. But I can handle it." I huddled up next to her and suddenly felt small without my blades and my secret pockets filled with poisons. I reminded myself that I wouldn't be needing them where I was going. There was a different kind of weapon I'd have to use to fight the Academy. Patience, wit, and using their own arrogance against them.

"It feels strange now," she said, her voice lowering. "You're really going to go to the Academy. Who would have thought it."

"Yep, well, here we are." I twisted to look out the window that gave us a bird's-eye view of the whitewashed castle that was Crown Princess Academy and the King's home.

Julianna turned with me and leaned back on her hands to gaze at the sleeping fortress. "Are you nervous?"

I shook my head. "No."

She swallowed. "Excited?"

I bit my cheek. "Resigned, perhaps." There was nothing I could say that would express the mixture of feelings swelling in my chest. I'd actually thought about this for a long time. Not attending the Academy, no, but how I would destroy the fae and their magic if they were ever stupid enough to let me inside.

7

LUCAS

y first task as Crown Prince wasn't to address the people of the realm, or peruse the current state of magic. No, nothing like that. I had to hop on a horse and personally collect the Princess Initiates of the Queen's Class. My father believed I should care for nothing more than which woman I would wed, who would bear my child and restore magic to one more member of our race.

I had no intention of continuing the barbaric practice. Sacrificing a human so that I might have a child with magic didn't solve my people's problem. My people were beyond saving and I had to stop them.

First, I had to play along until I could figure out a way to do so.

My first priority was to figure out which Crown Princess Initiate had illegally immigrated from the Dregs. Each crown shone like a beacon to my inner eye, showing me that all candidates were indeed inside the Kingdom among the Elites.

One of them would be the one I was looking for, one capable of bringing the whole system down.

She would be vile, wicked, and strong. Everything the Light feared.

Yet, none of the girls I'd met so far fit the part. Well, maybe a few were a bit wicked, even vile, but none of them were the Malice-friendly female I was looking for. All of the candidates introduced to me were typical Elites: Beautiful, graceful, and a bit snobbish. Perfect fae-fodder for anyone who wasn't me.

I was starting to lose hope when I realized the last stop was Rose Academy House. Odd place for a candidate for a role as prestigious as the Queen's Class.

"We've seemed to have run out of carriages," my human guard informed me, his voice steady but his eyes lowered in respect.

"How does a Kingdom run out of carriages?" I

pondered, not really caring, although we couldn't rightly drag the Princess Initiate behind my horse to take her the long ride back to the castle—although that image made me smirk.

The guard bobbed his head lower. "The Queen's Class has never numbered more than six members before. The King didn't tell me about the extra initiate."

Right, that was my fault.

I straightened as the Rose Academy House came into view, its pungent, sweet scent hitting me a moment later. The Houses loved to quite literally live up to their names. "It's no matter," I said, bored with him already. "She can't be that big. She'll ride with me."

The guard glanced at me briefly, his brown eyes flashing with worry before he looked down again. "Of course, sire."

The mansion parted its doors the instant our horse's hooves smacked against the golden streets bordering Rose Academy House. A woman with rosy red hair came out to greet us with a smile just as vibrant as her locks.

"Your Highness," she said, curtsying so low that I thought she might topple over, "you do us a great honor by your visit."

I frowned and hated that I was so recognizable. I much preferred my cowl and the snide looks I'd gotten in the Dregs to how Elites tripped over themselves in my presence. My fingers went to the glowing gold band on my forehead. I was an initiate of sorts myself and I wore the luxurious shackles to prove it.

"Is the Princess Candidate here?" I asked, ready to get on with it. If the girl I was looking for wasn't here, then I had to comb through the past twenty-four hours and figure out where I'd gone wrong.

The woman stared at my mouth and I realized my fangs had come out again. I couldn't help it. I was irritated.

Flinching, she bobbed her head up and down, sending her red curls flinging over her cleavage that was propped up so high it was a wonder she could breathe at all. "Yes, please, come inside and I will introduce her. We've prepared light nourishment before your return journey to the castle."

It was at least a two-hour ride back to the castle and I hadn't eaten anything all day. The other Houses knew better than to insult me with human food, however this was the Rose Academy House. They hadn't had a fae visitor in at least a generation and likely didn't know most fae would balk at the idea of "light nourishment."

Luckily for her, I wasn't like most fae and food sounded great to me.

My human guard followed me inside, his armor clinking heavily against his thighs in contrast to my own silent riding leathers. I had enough magic to protect me should trouble arise and had little use for weighty armor.

The Academy House hummed with resonance that matched my own magic, ancient fae having established this stronghold long before humans and Malice had come into the picture. It was why the Kingdom had been established on this wide circle of land with the Academy at the center. I had no doubt that the Academy itself held the key to the destruction of Malice.

So many secrets, so many mysteries. I had to be the one to unravel it in order to avenge my mother's death and stop a vicious cycle.

Two Elites greeted me at the foyer and I stopped when I met the gaze of a blonde girl in the glimmering pink dress. She boasted a tiny crown atop her head that marked her as a Princess Initiate, bonded with fae Light Magic and proof that the crown had made its choice. She radiated with Light, glittering with every movement. Her striking blue eyes matched my gaze without hesitation or the bubbly excitement that I'd seen from all the other girls.

There was something else there, too. Something I couldn't put my finger on.

Those eyes… could they be the ones that had watched me through wisps of Malice?

It wasn't possible… was it?

I have to be sure.

"May I introduce Lady Penelope, Princess Candidate, and Lady Julianna, a member of our House," the headmistress said as she ushered a servant to bring a platter of deep red fruit cut into rose petal shapes.

Cute.

Ignoring the delicacies and the girl in gold, I stepped closer to the blonde who rolled back her shoulders and continued to stare me down.

My guard cleared his throat, bouncing his gaze between the two of us, no doubt waiting for an unpleasant order.

I didn't move to discipline her. She was definitely not an Elite. An Elite would know such defiance would typically be met with a heavy hand across the cheek. This had to be the girl I was looking for.

A girl from the Dregs.

"I'm pleased to meet you," I offered, putting on my most charming smile. "Your dress suits you well."

Usually females melted when I turned on the charm, but not this one. Her eyes narrowed as if I'd just insulted her. Had I? The crown would have given her the dress it thought best suited a future Crown Queen, although now that I took a moment to give her a once over, she didn't stand like an Elite would with her chest popped out and hands clasped in front. Instead, she stood with her feet spread, her hands at her sides, and her intense gaze not missing a thing. Everything about her betrayed her origins.

The girl in gold nudged her, and the blonde seemed to flinch out of her fixation on me. "Uh, right, yes, thank you, I mean." Her eyelashes fluttered, making her look adorably attractive before she glanced at Lady Rose with a slight plea in her gaze. "Perhaps the Crown Prince would like some refreshments?"

I knew it was just a ploy to get me to stop staring at her, but I complied, turning to the tray of delicacies and selecting one of the rose-shaped biscuits and sniffed it. The composition reeked of butter, sugar, and flour; ingredients that would burn up in two seconds for fae metabolism and otherwise be quite useless in terms of nutrients. I popped the treat into my mouth anyway and the humans seemed to relax with relief. I chewed, mindful not to poke myself with my fangs, and offered a polite grin.

"If Your Highness would like more, we were preparing dinner for the House," Lady Rose began, her voice rising in excitement of the idea. I doubted any fae had accepted a dinner invitation in a hundred centuries. Even if Light Magic lived and breathed in the Kingdom in all things, including food ingredients, I still needed raw light to truly be sustained while outside of my realm.

I gave the headmistress a polite nod. "I'm afraid I must escort the Princess Candidate to the castle without further delay. Orientation includes dinner with the King."

The girl in gold gasped and nudged the female named Penelope. "The King? I told you!"

Penelope waved her away, glancing at me once with those eyes of blue steel that seemed to see right through me. "What if I don't want to go?" she asked, then poked at her crown. "This *thing* didn't really give me much of an option. Is that really how the candidates are chosen?"

My jaw slacked open and the servant next to me

stumbled, nearly tumbling the plate of delicacies all over me.

"Penelope!" Lady Rose screeched, her horror plain on her face. "We don't talk like that to the Crown Prince!" She snaked her fingers around the girl in gold, clenching the life from her wrist. A look I didn't understand exchanged between the pair. "You will attend to your duties or there will be… *consequences.*"

I held up a hand as I collected myself. "There'll be no need to be coarse. Isn't that right, Candidate Penelope?"

The female all but growled at me before nodding, causing a smirk to tug at the side of my mouth.

I think I found my girl.

This was a girl from the Dregs and I was going to use her to end what the fae had begun. The plan was already forming in my mind. If she was from the Dregs, if she was what I thought she was, then she had Malice somewhere in her body that could have survived her bonding with the Light.

She was the key to teaching my people a lesson— and revenge for what they'd done to my mother.

A lesson the fae will never forget.

8

PENNE

I didn't like the way that cocky fae looked at me. My efforts to anger him and see what he was really hiding had failed. I only seemed to amuse him. Emotions, especially of the darker nature such as rage or hurt, allowed me insight into someone's soul, and would have told me his secrets if he would just stop blasted... smirking.

I didn't know if my ability to read someone was a Malice thing or something I was just naturally good at, but it was worth a shot. Everyone was hiding something—an agenda, a secret, or something worse. I had no doubt that the Crown Prince was up to something and I was going to get to the bottom of it.

Unfortunately, my outburst had only served to

rile up Lady Rose and she was all the more eager to shove me out the door before the Crown Prince changed his mind about taking me to the Academy.

"Will you be able to reach me and let me know how it's going?" Jilly asked, holding both of my hands as tears streaked down her face.

I wasn't used to such open displays of empathy. Even in the Nest Jilly had always kept a strong face. I wasn't sure if that had been for my benefit or if that had been survival, but now when I was the one in danger Jilly didn't seem to be able to hold the tears back.

I don't cry. It must be this blasted crown... Making me go soft.

The unfamiliar sting in my own eyes made me swipe at them. "None of that, Jilly," I chided her and managed a smile. "I'm sure I'll be able to let you know, right, Your Highness?"

With a glance back at the Crown Prince, he offered a shrug. "We permit the rare letter, but only with the King's approval. The Academy is meant to be an immersive experience and it's best to keep loved ones at a distance while you're focusing on your studies."

A practical answer, but I was able to read between those lines. The King didn't want anyone knowing what really happened inside of the Academy, which gave me some insight as to why the Elites didn't fear it like they should. Maybe... just maybe, they had no idea what really went on behind closed doors.

One more truth I'll share with everyone when I bring the Academy down.

An ambitious goal, to be sure. The Academy had been a fixture of society ever since Malice had plagued humankind, but the one thing I'd learned about life was that the only constant was change.

The Crown Prince offered his hand to me, to which I returned a blank stare. "I could carry you to my horse if you insist on being stubborn." He smirked again, as if he would gain immense enjoyment from that. His eyes said: *Give me a reason, Princess.*

My fingers flinched, wanting to go for the dagger I kept strapped to my thigh. Instead, I bunched my dress enough so I could walk down the short steps to the street without tumbling over my feet. How did the Elites walk around in these ridiculous outfits? It was no wonder their females were so stunted.

Maybe that'll give me an edge at the Academy.

As if sensing my wariness, the Prince took a step closer. "Shall we, my dear?"

"I'm capable of walking, thank you," I said, turning my nose up in what I hoped was an appropriately snooty gesture for an Elite.

He laughed again and Lady Rose turned pale. "You plan on walking all the way to the Academy?" he asked. "That would be a full day's trek."

"So?"

One glance at the horrified look on Lady Rose's face told me walking to the Academy would not be customary. So, how did they travel around here? They'd brought horses, but one was an overly decorated stallion clearly intended for the Crown Prince and the other was for his guard who'd already mounted and was giving us worried looks.

"Is there no carriage?" Lady Rose offered, twisting her lips so they formed what I guessed was supposed to be a polite smile.

"My apologies, my lady," the guard said with a bow of his head. "There seems to have been a complication, so the Crown Prince has graciously offered that the Candidate ride one of our horses with us."

What?

Oh, Malice...

The Crown Prince took my hand without warning, drawing me closer to him. I squeaked in surprise and instinct made me delve down where my Malice usually lived to fling him off, but instead of the cold comfort of my power I was met with an unfamiliar flash of heat.

Ouch...

The tiny crown on my head hummed with disapproval and the fae's silver eyes flinched in my direction, betraying that he'd noticed the attempt. "That won't work, not until you understand your magic," he whispered, his voice pitched low so only I could hear him.

Malice... Can he feel my magic?

I studied him, trying to figure out if he was referring to the Light the crown pushed into my body, or the Malice that I kept locked away in my heart. If he knew about my Malice, then allowing him to take me to the Academy was just as good as a death sentence—wasn't it? Was he just putting on a polite face until he got me behind bars for dismemberment, or worse?

"Light magic is new to me," I offered, testing him. I raised my hand and ran a delicate touch over the crown atop my head. It seemed to purr from the contact. "Will the Academy teach me how to use it?"

He smiled, the effect so charming on his handsome face that I nearly forgot I was supposed to fear him. "I will personally teach you how to use magic, if you so wish."

Not what I expected.

He laced his fingers and crouched, giving me a stepping stool to get onto his horse. He looked at me expectantly until I gently placed my glittering pink slipper into his waiting grip and leveraged myself over the massive beast.

I realized too late that the dress would make it impossible for me to straddle the horse like I wanted to. I'd never seen such a creature before, but my instinct told me to mimic the human guard who sat atop his horse and looked so regal.

Me? Not regal. Definitely.

When I couldn't swing my leg over, I nearly toppled over the saddle before the fae grabbed me around my hips and steadied me, his strong grip making me flinch.

I was not used to being touched.

He chuckled. "Don't be so stiff. This is going to be a long ride if you're squeamish from a little physical contact." He placed his foot in the golden stirrup and launched himself over the beast with ease, straddling the saddle behind me and inching me closer to his chest. Before I could protest, he wrapped one arm securely around my middle and the other took the reins. He clicked his tongue and the horse moved under us, making me grab onto the first thing I could to keep from losing my balance—which happened to be the fae's muscular arm that flexed around my waist, keeping me pinned against him.

"Be sure to write!" Jilly called, waving goodbye and oblivious of my horror that I was being manhandled by the Crown Prince.

Lady Rose ushered Jilly inside and I noticed for the first time that the streets were completely empty, but after a moment through the jostling of the horse's movements I spotted moving curtains in windows and curious eyes peering through crystal glass.

No cheering. No parades. Just fearful stares behind the protection of golden walls.

The Kingdom is like a prison—and I'm sitting with the warden.

I'd never thought of the Kingdom that way, but when I relaxed enough to look over the horizon I saw how Malice closed in on every corner of the glorious city, it made me feel trapped like I never had before.

The horse turned away from the dark perimeter

and clopped its way down a single street that ended in the forest that surrounded the Academy. The glorious castle itself was visible atop a hill, parading over the surrounding greenery with its whitewashed perfection. I blinked when a rainbow crested over the pinnacle.

"Ah," the prince said, his voice a pleasant rumble against my senses, "the Academy welcomes the final Princess Candidate to her new home."

I swallowed hard and dug my fingers into his forearm as the horse lurched us towards the polished castle.

"The name's Penne," I corrected him, my voice coming out strained, so I cleared it and tried again. "Not Penelope, not Princess Candidate—Penne."

He chuckled, the sound rolling over me like a caress. "Penne," he said as if testing the word on his tongue. His arm around my middle squeezed and his breath puffed against my neck. "You can call me Lucas."

Heat thrummed from my crown in response, leaving a tingling sensation surging through my entire body—although if it was responding to his magic, or just the effect he was having on me, I wasn't sure.

Malice... this fae's going to be trouble.

9

PENNE

When we first started our route through the forest, Lucas only managed to keep me on the horse by clutching me around the waist. His arm grazed the lump that was my blade strapped to my thigh. I could almost feel his curiosity.

"Care to share what's so bulky underneath this dress of yours?" he asked with an amused tone.

I flattened my lips, determined not to respond. Surely most ladies didn't have blades hidden underneath frills and lace, but I couldn't think of a good reply. So, silence it was. Maybe if I ignored him he'd just leave me alone about it.

He shifted me to hold the reins and my weight with one hand while he jerked up the hem of my dress with the other. I screeched and slapped him away—or tried to. I wasn't in the best position to deal much damage, and I couldn't very well use my Malice on him, either.

"I'm not stupid, Candidate. You have a weapon and I intend to disarm you before you hurt yourself with it."

Rage seethed over me as he slipped the blade from its simple sheath. "The only one I'd be hurting is you," I snapped.

He chuckled as he inspected the blade, holding it up the light. It was a fine blade, one I'd used ever since I had joined the Northern Sector Guild. I'd gotten a nice sum from my first job and I had used it to buy that blade. It's not like it had true sentimental value, but it signified the day that I took my life in my own hands.

I didn't like Lucas messing with it.

"Unusual," he remarked, then surprised me by hefting the blade towards me, careful not to slice either of us as the horse moved. "Perhaps I'm being rude. If you would feel better having the dagger, then go on, take it."

Was this a test? Or maybe he was just toying with me.

"Just keep it," I snapped, gripping the sides of the

saddle, wanting to find something to hold onto that was anywhere except his steady, muscular arm. "It was silly of me to bring it."

He made a thoughtful sound, then sheathed the dagger in his boot. "Very well. I'll hold onto it for you, until you're ready to reclaim it."

Irritated beyond recourse, I bit my tongue and decided not to speak to him again for the rest of the ride. He was definitely toying with me.

I decided that I did not like Lucas, although that came as no surprise. I'd never gotten along with Elites, much less the fae. I dealt better with ruffians and Malice Casters that at least knew who I was and the ramifications of annoying me.

Lucas had no such qualms.

"What's life like at the Academy House?" he asked, breaking the hour-long silence accentuated only by the muffled hoofbeats against the dirt road.

I squirmed, still trapped in his iron grip. "Dull," I said, hoping he would drop the subject. Ironically, I was never a good liar. Never needed to be. Hiding was my thing. And the occasional stabbing. I pushed that attractive thought out of my mind. "What's life like in the Fae Realm?"

He chuckled. "It's rather like this forest. It's so full of life, but you can't tell unless you know where to look." He pointed at a glimmer of color between the mesh of trees. "Do you see those butterflies? Those are magical butterflies that only come to life when a Princess Candidate comes through these woods."

We were so deep in the forest that I'd lost myself in watching the wildlife and spectral creatures that guarded the mystical woods. They were hard to spot, but I noticed them like shadows shifting behind leaves and branches. Maybe the average human would have had trouble spotting life in this forest, but not me. I thrived in darkness and knew how to find life in the most unlikely of places.

The butterflies, though, I would have missed the delicate blues and oranges and dismissed them as tricks of the light if the fae hadn't pointed them out. "Magical butterflies," I said, my voice flat. Was I supposed to be impressed? "Like conjurations?" Even though the butterflies were beautiful and glittered like lost starlight in the shadows, they were nothing like Zizi. They didn't have her charm or her wit—just pointless decorations on an evergreen tapestry.

"Yes, that's exactly what they are," he said with a sense of approval that made me regret my slip. "You'll learn to conjure creatures of your own. Does that interest you?"

"Not particularly," I said, trying to sound bored. "I don't see how making butterflies would be useful."

I was probably pushing him a little too much, but he was getting on my nerves. And I really disliked the idea of wasting magic on frivolous things such as conjuring butterflies.

Instead of bristling, he rewarded me with another chuckle, the sound sending vibrations through my body. I shivered, wishing I was anywhere else except on this horse with his body so close to mine. As a Malice Caster, no one ever invaded my personal space, but the Crown Prince seemed immune to whatever element I possessed that typically warded the male gender away.

As his grip around my waist shifted, settling my weight better against him, I dumbly recalled that I was a potential wife for him. If I graduated Crown Princess Academy and became the Crown Princess, then that would mean…

No, not even going there, because I was going to dismantle the Academy before I became anyone's wife—and if it did come to that, I'd dismantle his face.

"I suppose you could make something else," he mused, his arm flexing around me, shifting me with ease and betraying how strong he really was. He held my weight so effortlessly as the horse jostled us. The fae Prince compensated my lack of balance in my precarious side-saddle position with his own perfect harmony with the beast's movements, irritating me all the more. "What would you like to make?"

I narrowed my eyes at the butterflies as they followed us through the forest, lining our path with blues and oranges that glittered and left drifting motes of magical dust. Now that we were talking about them, the creatures were showing off. "What about a weapon?" I mused, intrigued by how he would react by something so brutish. If he saw I wasn't princess quality, perhaps he'd stop being so interested in me.

The Crown Prince barked a laugh—not what I expected—and our human guard ahead of us twitched. The male sent one wayward glance full of worry that told me I was definitely walking a thin line.

Seeming assured that I was still in one piece, the guard kneed his horse and trotted on ahead of us, my guess was to get out of earshot so he wouldn't be held accountable as a witness if the Crown Prince decided I wasn't amusing anymore.

"A weapon," the voice at my neck almost purred. "Would you know how to use it?"

"Of course," I snapped, then bit my tongue hard enough to flinch. I was falling right into his silken-voice trap.

"Do they teach weapon-skill at Rose Academy?" he mused, ducking when a low hanging branch barred our path, the motion fitting his chin into the crook of my neck.

Malice... how long is this horse ride?

He didn't pull away when the path was clear.

"No," I said, hating how defensive I sounded, "but it can't be that hard. Pointy end goes into the bad guy." I made a jabbing motion with my fist to demonstrate.

He rewarded me with another warm chuckle and I knew that this fae was pushing all of my buttons—both good and bad ones. A slick sense of magic tingled over my skin at his proximity, the effect as intoxicating as the puffs of breath against my cheek. He could kill me with a mere thought, could reveal his true nature and destroy me from the inside out... but I also sensed an intrigue between us that went both ways. I had survived the worst of the Dregs, but I'd never met my match. Something about the danger of him thrilled me and made me want to test his boundaries.

"I look forward to our sparring sessions, then," he

said, finally pulling away enough for me to breathe, but he kept one arm securely around my body to keep me from falling.

I couldn't help myself and chuckled. "Part of the Academy includes sparring?" Now that was a class I could get on board with.

He hummed in acknowledgment, the sound agonizingly charming. "Yes, and I have to say I'm looking forward to it."

I stiffened. He sounded so cocky, as if he thought I was just an Academy House girl he could play with like a doll. If he thought he could best me in a sparring session, he was in for a nasty surprise. "That makes two of us."

"Adorable. Truly, little Candidate." When I growled, he ignored me and pointed down the dusty path to an opening in the lush greenery. "We're almost there."

The horses picked up their pace, as if eager to rid themselves of the magical forest. The pale beasts weren't as comfortable in darkness as I was, but I didn't blame them. The break of sunlight opened up to the spectacle of the castle, revealing massive marble columns that glittered with fae magic and a rainbow crested overhead in welcome.

Looks like I was home.

10

LUCAS

A two-hour horse ride with the unruly female locked in my arms was almost more torture than I could bear. The scent of roses and sunlight clung to her, teasing me until I couldn't resist just a moment with my nose pressed behind her ear to inhale the intoxicating allure of her. Her magic called to me and made me want to forget all my qualms about fae-kind morality and embrace her as the future Crown Princess and Queen.

All the more reason I had to resist.

This was a girl from the Dregs. I didn't know how she'd posed as a member of Rose Academy House or how she'd gotten the crown to accept her, but she had Malice hidden deep beneath the layers of fae magic that gave her skin a golden glow. It was faint, and if I hadn't known to look for it and have an excuse to have her pressed up against me during the long ride, I would have missed it entirely… but it was there.

Malice.

Darkness.

Danger.

I watched her as the guard helped her dismount, her warmth leaving my skin cold and my body yearning. I clamped down hard on the instinct that was driving me and teased at the crown at my brow that was no doubt fueling my desires. Magic wanted me to take a queen, wanted me to pick my favorite among the selection and assist the candidates in their classes.

Which was precisely why I had to make sure she failed.

Every.

Single.

Class.

Not only would that prevent me from getting too close to her, but it would feed her with enough Malice to accomplish the task ahead. If she could survive what I was going to put her through, she would be a time bomb the fae wouldn't see coming. A candidate full of Malice sent through a portal to the Fae Realm? Yeah, that would definitely break down the portal for good and stop this madness. Fae weren't supposed to be here. This world could finally start to heal if the festering source was removed.

I adjusted my boot in the stirrup and swung myself off the beast, patting its neck before approaching the castle with Penelope marching ahead of me. Of course she didn't wait for my arm —a girl from the Dregs didn't need a princely escort.

At least she looked the part she played as an Elite as she entered the foyer and stopped momentarily to gaze up at the grand architecture full of swirling designs the fae favored. Her long, graceful form drew my eye over her body, admiring her curves and the delicate lift of her nose.

A servant greeted us with a silver platter with one lonely invitation in a sealed envelope. I caught a hint of giggling girl students escaping down the hall, no doubt trying to catch a glimpse of the final Candidate for the Queen's Class. I could have used my magic to identify them and report them for negative marks, but the innocent mirth of the younger students amused me, so I pretended I hadn't noticed.

"Princess Candidate," he drawled, bowing low and offering the plate. "The Crown King and the other candidates await you in the dining hall."

Instead of taking the offering, she stared as if he'd just invited her to eat off the floor. "Dining hall? I've just been on a horse for two hours and I have forest grime all over me. Can't I wash up?" Her eyes said she could care less about "washing up," but it was a good ploy if she wanted a moment alone to decide her next move.

The servant didn't budge and stared at her with his tray still elevated. "I'm afraid you're quite late, Candidate. There will be time to wash up after the meal."

She bristled and glanced back at me as if this were somehow my fault. Scoffing with indignance that was worthy of her fake station, she snatched up the letter and ripped it open and read it aloud. "You're invited to join the Crown King and your fellow Candidates for the Orientation Meal." She rolled her eyes and slapped the letter against her thigh—which made her pink dress flutter around her long legs. I couldn't help but notice the way her dress cinched around her middle, hugging her hips along its seductive curves. Holy fae, she was gorgeous. "Really? You needed to hand me a letter for that?"

The servant kept a deadpan face, but a bulge at his temple as he locked his jaw betrayed she was getting on his nerves. That amused me.

The servant glanced at me.

Oops, were my fangs out again?

He motioned down the hall. "This way, if you please."

I cleared my throat and offered my arm to Penelope. "Perhaps I can take the blame," I suggested with my most alluring smile.

Seemingly unaffected by charms that typically made females melt, she glared, her blue eyes burning with a fire that I wanted to tame. "You're the one who brought me here. Not like I could have come on my own. So yeah, you're taking the blame."

She was right, of course. She couldn't have hoped to get to the Academy without a magically endowed escort. The forest might have accepted us, but that was only because the magic in our crowns evaded the protective wards that surrounded the Castle. The carriages helped to amplify the effect, although since I had a crown of my own we were safe enough. The forest comprised of beasts and nightmares, both of

Malice and of Light that were the fae's best kept secret.

I just hoped she didn't decide to run and uncover those fatal secrets for herself.

She looped her arm through mine and set her gaze forward. "Let's get this over with."

11

PENNE

*T*he last thing I wanted to do was endure a formal dinner. Thanks to my upbringing, I could go days without eating. I wasn't sure if that was a boon of being a Malice Caster or if I was just used to starvation, but the instant the sickeningly sweet scents of meat and pastries hit my nose, my stomach clenched with rebellion and all I wanted to do was stuff my face with the colorful array of delicacies.

I licked my lips, then stopped myself, recognizing the wave of warm magic running from my head to my toes.

Stupid crown wanted me to get fat. I sniffed the air, taking note of foreign elements that rang my warning bells. Bet the meal was laced with fae magic and would only indenture me to this place if I ate enough.

My stomach growled again—loudly.

The fae Prince smirked at me. Cocky bastard.

I took a moment to take in the long table that housed a row of straight-spined females with tiny crowns atop their heads. Each sat primly in a glittering gown that complimented my own, different only slightly in style and in color. The females stared at me, none of them having touched their over-flowing plates. I realized that the Princess Candidates were arranged in order of the colors of the rainbow. A spot was left open between red and orange—the closest seats near the Crown King matched by an empty throne at his side. The King watched me expectantly as I swallowed.

I glanced up at Lucas, wondering if he was really going to abandon me to my seat. He gave me a charming smile, which made me flinch because I realized he had them out again… those fangs. I didn't see fae with elongated canines outside of the few prisoners we'd managed to take in the Northern Sector. Fangs were typically a show of aggression, but in Lucas' case, I sensed that it meant something else.

I think I… excited him.

Gross.

Catching my gaze dipping to his mouth, he ran his tongue over one sharp fang, the motion somehow lewd and alluring at the same time.

Glowering, I untangled myself from his arm and took my seat. By the looks of abhorrence on the girls' faces, I might as well have spit in the Crown Prince's face.

Lucas took the empty throne and the King released a long sigh. "Glad you have decided to grace us with your presence, son." He glanced at me, disapproval clear in his gaze. "You as well, young Candidate."

I gave a bow of my head and folded my hands in my lap. The plate of food beneath my nose made my mouth water, but I didn't dare reach for a scrumptious bite.

The girl to my left hissed at me, "Take your napkin."

Glancing at her, I noted that she had neatly folded a napkin across their legs, so I took mine and did the same.

The King released another sigh before he stood, seemingly already exasperated with me. His chair screeched across the marble floors, the sound obnoxious in the otherwise somber and elegant room. For a fae, he wasn't very graceful.

In fact, if it hadn't been for the pointed ears that reached his elaborate crown, as well as his tall stature when he straightened to his full height, I wouldn't have guessed him to be a fae at all. Perhaps his time in the Kingdom had changed him.

A long beard puffed around his surprisingly rugged features and his gaze held a hardness that I'd only seen in the Dregs. The King might have gone numb over a past trauma, or he'd lost something emotionally valuable to him. Assuming fae had emotions, of course.

There was the Queen, I wondered. Everyone knew that she'd been dispatched years prior, which could make a king lonely, perhaps.

Like most queens, she'd had her reign, then when she'd started to show signs of illness from the heavy toll of magic her role took on her, she'd been given a one-way ticket to the Fae Realm for the promised rejuvenation.

The icy coldness in the King's eyes spoke of a different truth—one that I knew all too well.

She was dead.

I knew it because I'd seen it over and over again in the Dregs. Humans could hardly survive Malice, much less a human infused with fae magic. I suspected Light magic wasn't so different in that regard. I didn't know how the King had used her, or why, but it didn't matter. All that mattered was that I wasn't going to let it happen again.

As if he could sense my plotting, Lucas gave me a sideways glance and shook his head so slightly that I would have missed it had it not been for the jolt of magical warning that zapped through my veins.

What the Malice was that?

The stern look on Lucas's face said that I'd better keep quiet or he'd buzz me again.

"Chosen candidates of the Academy's Queen's Class, I greet you," the King began, his voice booming across the dining hall and settling uncomfortably in my chest.

My tiny crown preened at the sound of his voice, making my skin and dress shimmer. I noted the same impact on the other girls as they straightened and turned their attention to the rugged fae.

"Every class at the Academy has a vital role in our Kingdom's society," he explained. "Graduates serve by pushing back the Malice that invades this world and further secures the Kingdom's boundaries, after which taking up residence in the Fae Realm, a true honor."

A low hum of excitement sounded through the group.

"The Queen's Class, especially," the King continued, "will produce the most vital and powerful of graduates yet."

"Isn't there only one graduate?" I asked, unable to bite my tongue.

All eyes swerved to me.

Lucas rubbed his temples.

The King studied me before responding. "If you mean will there be only one Crown Princess, that is correct, but it is entirely possible for there to be multiple graduates, just as any other class."

"Has there ever been multiple graduates from a Queen's Class?" I pressed. I didn't want these other girls to be blindsighted by the gruesome truth. They deserved to know what they were getting into.

When he didn't answer, a few of my neighbors paled.

Dismissing my question with a wave of his hand, he rolled his shoulders back and swept his dark gaze over us. It gave me the sensation of being in a herd of cattle just told it was about to be slaughtered, all for the greater good, of course. "Rest assured, the Queen's Class is the most challenging—yet the most rewarding—class at the Academy," the King continued. "Without our graduates, the Kingdom would not exist."

"Nor the House of Embers," said a girl in a red dress, raising her chin to the King.

He regarded her with a nod of approval. "Yes, the House of Embers is closest to the outskirts. There was an incident of Malice infestation only a year ago, I believe."

She nodded, sending waves of red hair curling over her naked shoulders. Her dress hugged her bodice and I wondered how she could even breathe in the thing. "It was terrible," she said, shivering. "I'd never seen anything like it. Then the Academy showed up and blasted the shadows with Light. It was... extraordinary." Her eyes sparkled with the memory.

I raised a brow at that. I'd heard about Malice slipping past Kingdom defenses last year, but I'd been under the impression that the fae had rein-forced the shield that kept Malice out of the Kingdom—not humans.

If there really were surviving Academy graduates, I wanted to meet them.

"Would it be possible for graduates to train us?" I asked, feeling braver now that I wasn't the only one asking questions.

The King gave me a nod. "In time, once you have proven yourself, that would be possible."

I had so many questions. If there really were survivors, did they live in the Fae Realm now? Did that mean they could tell me how to travel between worlds, or how realm magic worked? That opened up so many more opportunities than just taking down the Academy. If I could eliminate fae travel to and from the human world—

"We take great pride in maintaining Academy secrecy," the King added, interrupting my thoughts. "Very few know the true extent of the power granted to those who graduate, and it's best that we keep it that way so that you may train and work without distraction." He frowned. "If the ruffians of this world knew of the power you will attain here, they would stop at nothing to burn down the sacred forest and use you, and your new gifts, for themselves."

I curled my fingers underneath the table, bunching up my nauseatingly pink dress. He meant the Dreg-dwellers—the very people he had written off as too inconsequential to protect. Of course people like Gavin would come for the Academy if they knew what kind of power was here. Malice, he probably already knew and that's why he was so focused on manipulating Elites.

That surge of warning hit me again, Lucas' gaze finding mine and filling me with a sense of dread.

Then I noticed the King was watching me and I wiped away the sweat forming at my brow.

"Do you have something to add, Candidate…" he consulted a list on the table, "Penelope?"

I ground my teeth, using all my willpower not to correct him that I preferred to be called Penne.

I would have patted myself on the back for that restraint had my mouth not opened and blurted the next thing I wanted to say. "If the Academy and its graduates are so powerful, then why hide behind an enchanted forest at all? Why leave the Dregs defenseless and watch Malice orphan and kill hundreds of humans every year?"

I might have come to an understanding with the Malice in myself, but that didn't mean I had forgotten what it was. It was danger, darkness, and death all in one terrible little package that continued to decimate what was left of mankind.

What had been an excited murmur descended into a shocked hush across the table.

Yep, me and my big mouth.

The King surprised me by giving me a grin—

although the lengthening canines poking out of his mouth suggested I was pushing my luck. "Lucas, where did you say you found Candidate Penelope?"

"Rose Academy House," Lucas immediately supplied, flinching his gaze forward.

So, even the Crown Prince was afraid of this fae.

That should have scared me, instead, it just made me dig my heels in more—or should I say, made me do a more thorough job of digging my own grave. "This isn't about me," I snapped. "This is about what you're telling us we're supposed to do. We're supposed to *stop* Malice, right? If I'm Crown Queen, I can tell you right now that I will protect everyone I can—not just the Kingdom."

One of the girls gripped her glass of golden bubbling liquid, looking like she wanted to take a long gulp, but she didn't move.

Another, the one in red, gave me a wicked smile. Maybe she thought I'd already eliminated myself as competition.

"You're not Crown Queen, *Candidate*, not yet," the King said, his fangs lengthening far enough to reach the bottom of his chin as his words slurred around the massive tusks, "and you have a long way to go to prove yourself before you can start barking declarations about things you don't yet understand."

I looked at Lucas to see if he might defend me. If he was supposed to be my future husband in this screwed up arrangement, surely he wouldn't let anyone talk to me that way, not even the King. Yet, he didn't even flinch in my direction as he kept his gaze locked on an invisible point at the end of the long table.

Coward.

The King snarled, his words turning more beast-like than human. "You start at the beginning like everyone else—here, at orientation. The crowns choose their Candidates carefully, so I will trust in our Fae magic that your misplaced loyalties will be rectified soon enough." He grabbed his glass and raised it, displaying that it glowed with magic. I realized it was liquid Light, a raw substance that would set someone up for a lifetime in Dregs. "I make this toast to the Queen's Class, may you be worthy of the role it offers." He knocked back the contents in one fluid motion.

The rest of the girls seemed relieved that the King hadn't made me implode at my seat—except maybe the girl in red who glowered at me. They all brought their glasses to their plump lips. While the liquid wasn't filled with Light magic like the King's, it seemed to calm them.

Lucas didn't touch his and continued to stare at that invisible spot.

My nose twitched, an old skill startling me, proving that my Malice wasn't completely buried.

I smelled… fear.

Grabbing my glass, I sniffed the contents. The scent of strawberries and sunlight made my mouth water, but I sensed magic in it, too. Not Light magic… something else.

The King growled. "Don't disrespect this table. Finish the toast to the last drop. That includes you, Candidate Penelope."

Hurrying to obey, the girls gulped down their glasses and I reluctantly sipped mine. Warmth tingled pleasantly down my throat and I didn't sense anything invasive or wrong with the drink. My Malice had a knack for letting me know if someone was trying to poison me, and plus, it wouldn't make much sense for the King to poison the newly appointed Queen's Class.

As if to refute that conclusion, one of the girls who'd finished her glass grabbed her throat and began to sputter. Her eyes widened and she looked to the King as if he might help her. She opened her mouth to speak, but a gurgle came out as dark, jagged lines slashed across her delicate skin. The sickness wrapped over her arms, across her face, and turned her eyes black.

Malice.

I looked down at my own glass, two gulps short of being empty, and then a hard hand slammed down on the table. "Finish it!" Bellowed the King as he drew a blade from his belt, "or I will finish *all* of you."

I had no doubt he was serious. If there was Malice in my glass, then the joke was on him. Malice and I had an understanding.

I knocked back the last of the contents and swallowed, then gave him a glare of defiance.

Then... the icy burn came.

Buckling over, I gripped my chest where the foreign Malice rampaged through my body. Malice could be cold or uncomfortable, but it had never felt like this, like jagged blades ripping their way through my insides. I realized as heat exploded at the top of my head that the tiny crown was pumping me with Light, desperately trying to burn out the Malice.

No, you stupid crown! I screamed my thoughts at it. I had to *accept* the Malice, not destroy it.

While I worked my own internal battle, the girls around me glowed with white-hot Fae magic, their dresses glimmering with fierce power and their eyes glazing over as they struggled to burn away the Malice in their bodies.

One by one, each of them sizzled the darkness away into nothing—except for one, the petite girl at my side in a dress that had once been a lovely orange but now was turning grey. Her eyes swirled with darkness as she latched onto my arm.

"Help me," she croaked, fear naked on her features.

I gripped her shoulders and tried to draw her Malice into myself, but my stupid crown was fighting me and I was still trying to get it to stop shredding the Malice I'd ingested.

Accept the Malice, I instructed it. *Allow it inside. Put it in the lock in my chest—that's where it'll stay.*

The crown burned atop my head so hot that I was sure my hair was about to catch on fire, but it finally listened to me, about the Malice in my own body at least, and pushed it into the jagged scar in my chest. I winced as knives crossed the barrier to the scar over my heart, but then the Malice settled and I felt a little less like I was going to die.

The girl in my arms, though, wilted and I couldn't rip the Malice out of her. The blasted crown wouldn't let me.

I snarled and clutched the girl to my chest. Her cheek pressed against my skin, a cold clammy reminder that I was already too late. "Lucas!" I screeched at the Crown Prince who had picked up his fork and was pushing food around on his plate. "Do something, you blasted fae!"

The King chuckled at my outrage and rested a heavy hand on his son's shoulder. "Already on a first name basis with this one?"

Lucas lifted one lip in a snarl, revealing painfully long canines. "She got the wrong idea because she rode my horse here. She'll have to pass classes like all the rest before I'll respond to anything other than my title."

The King patted his son's back. "Agreed."

My mouth dropped open as rage fueled my body, but then a fatigue took me so strong that black spots trickled across my vision.

"An impressive pass rate," the King announced as he took his seat again and picked up a fork, taking in the survivors of the toast. All the girls struggled to stay upright in their seats, their crowns burning bright as they worked out the Malice in their bodies. "This meal will sustain you from the high levels of magic you have just used to demonstrate your worthiness to be a part of this class." He jabbed the fork into a chunk of meat and shoved it into his mouth. When we all stared, he jerked a hand with impatience. "Eat!" he barked around the bite.

The girls flinched and began eating, leaving me with the girl gone cold in my arms.

"Lucas," I hissed again, and this time he acknowledged me with eyes so blue that the ice I saw in them rivaled the Malice I'd absorbed into my chest.

"You heard the King," he growled, making no attempt to retract his fangs as he wiped his mouth with his napkin, tearing the fine fabric. "Eat. And until further notice, you are to call me Crown Prince."

I'd never seen anyone look at me the way that human looked at me. It made me…

Angry.

Excited.

Terrified.

Maybe it was because for the first time in my life I witnessed someone challenge a fae like my father. It was something I'd always wanted to do—but I wasn't an idiot.

But really?

She was just being ridiculous.

It wasn't possible to save the entire world—the fae had tried that once before and look what happened. We'd lost our magic. It took a Kingdom and indentured servitude of the surviving humans to keep our magic in the royal bloodlines. The Academy was a fortress and last resort to keep the fae in power.

It wasn't right. The fae who pulled the political strings didn't deserve to live, my father included. There was an entire council in the Fae Realm that I couldn't get to, but I didn't need to. I just needed to stop *them* from getting *here.*

It would leave humanity unprotected, but from what I've seen, they did better without our "protection." Humanity could survive Malice—I'd seen it myself in the Dregs. The fae, for all our strengths, would be ruined forever if allowed to continue down this path.

The Academy needed to be shut down and the link between worlds broken.

It would be the only way to help my people go back to their roots and let go of the power-hungry obsession I'd seen in my father's eyes. At least, if they could accept life without magic, without the very thing that made us near-immortal and powerful, perhaps they could be saved.

Maybe I was fooling myself and there was too much corruption. Perhaps the fae could never be rescued from themselves, but I found I didn't really care. Not after so much suffering by our hands. The evidence of how far gone the fae were displayed itself before me. Penelope clung to the now lifeless body. The girl in her arms slumping and Penelope readjusted her weight, pulling her closer to her chest as she continued to try and... what was she trying to do?

I realized the truth when shadows flickered around her fingertips and panic seized my chest.

Holy fae... she *was* the Malice Caster I'd seen in the Dregs. She was trying to suck the Malice out of the lifeless body now in her arms and into herself. Stupid, stupid girl.

I snapped my fingers at the waiting butler who also doubled as security. We knew what these girls would be capable of, even if they didn't know it themselves yet. If anything, we needed protection from them once they learned to master the Light in their bodies. "Take the girl away," I ordered, keeping my tone flat. Penelope's head snapped up, her eyes going wide with indignation.

The butler moved to her side and offered a hand. "Please, Candidate. She is already gone."

She drew in a deep breath, flicking her gaze between me and the butler. "You're monsters!" she screeched and clung to the body even tighter. Light flickered in her gaze and I wondered if she was already coming to terms with her new powers—if so, this was about to get very interesting.

My father watched with a sense of bored amusement. He'd been to countless orientation dinners and seen girls fail to snuff out the small bit of Malice fed to them to test their instinctual control over Fae magic. Magical instinct could not be taught and this was the most efficient way to know whose skills to hone and who would be a lost cause.

Brutal, but the way of the fae.

I knew if my father decided Penelope was no longer entertaining he would add her to the list of failures whether her instinct over magic was impressive or not.

That meant I had to take matters into my own hands. I put on a show of getting up from my seat and glowering before reaching her and snatching away the lifeless form. It broke my heart to be so coarse, but this was the only way to keep her safe. "Stop making a fool of yourself," I snarled.

The look of hatred she awarded me with said that she would never forgive me for this—no matter my intentions. She couldn't possibly know that I was trying to save her life, but even if she did, I doubted that she would care.

"Sit, eat, and do as you're told," I added for good

measure before cradling the girl's body in my arms and passing her to the butler. "The girl will receive a proper burial in the Fae Realm. Now go, take her to the gates."

All the girls watched with wide eyes as the butler took the body away.

Penelope, eyes blazing with magic and rage, ground her teeth before taking her seat. She took up a fork and stabbed a piece of meat, her grip trembling as she lifted the morsel to her mouth. She looked up at me, those wild eyes proving to me that she could never be tamed.

"You were right," she snapped.

I tilted my head. "About?"

She turned her attention back to her plate as her brows pushed together. "When you said that I have a lot to learn, you were right. But don't worry, I'm a quick study."

A faint smile hinted at my lips. I was counting on that.

13

PENNE

After enduring a tasteless dinner, I was escorted to my chambers. It was hard not to miss the whispers and pointing from other students as I made my walk of shame behind my handmaiden. It rubbed me the wrong way how they seemed too complacent, as if someone hadn't just died.

To add to matters, my room was far too luxurious for a prison. I would have preferred iron bars and a bed of straw that more appropriately marked this place for what it was. Instead, each Crown Princess Candidate was awarded an oversized room with colors that matched her crown's selection of the rainbow and a plethora of cushy furniture to go with it.

So, naturally, my room had enough pink to give me a headache.

I groaned and eased onto the bed and wished the maidservant at the door would stop pestering me that she could wash my hair for me or give me a foot massage.

"A girl is dead," I reminded her. "So… no to the massage."

Looking pale, the maidservant's gaze flicked to the floor and she folded her hands in front of her dress. "Oh, right, Orientation Dinner. It can be a bit hard the first time."

Sighing, I clutched the edge of the bed. "How long have you worked here?"

She bit her lip before replying. "Three years. It's the greatest honor to be maidservant to a Candidate of the Queen's Class." She glanced at me, fight in her gaze that hadn't been there a moment before. "I'm going to earn back my place at the Academy, no matter what it takes."

That made my brows shoot up. "What?"

She straightened and a sense of regality swept over her that I hadn't noticed before. "Before I came to the Academy I was Lady Olivia of the Willow House, but now you can just call me Olli. My House is not well known, and I'm afraid I wasn't properly prepared for the skills required to graduate from the Academy. I was a student, but my scores dipped too low." She shrugged. "If you survive long enough, then I'll get another chance and I'll join next season's classes anew."

"I see." I was glad to hear that death wasn't the only alternative for failing classes at Crown Princess Academy, although I wasn't sure how I felt about her fate being linked to mine, or how casually she admitted I could die.

She bobbed with a short curtsey. "If there's nothing else that you need, I will confirm your class with the registrar and work out your schedule for the week. Things can be a bit… tumultuous during the transition." She glanced at the crown atop my head and a flash of envy crossed her gaze.

I wasn't sure if I could count Olli as an ally, but I definitely wanted to be alone, so I gave her a nod. "Very well. Thank you for your, uh, help."

She gave me a polite smile. "I've already set out hot stones for your bath and should you need anything else, simply ring one of the bells with my name on them." She tapped her ear. "I'll hear it no matter where I am." She waited for my nod before sweeping out of the room and gently closing the door behind her.

Releasing a long breath, I endured a long look at my room, skimming over one of the bells that Olivia had pointed out. A magical ping service for my handmaiden? Ridiculous.

In spite of the pink nonsense, it was definitely the nicest room I'd ever stayed in. A wide window allowed plenty of sunlight to stream through, although the light was dimming and night settled a red dusky glow over the courtyard outside and gave my room a bloody tone. Somehow that felt appropriate. Yet it was impossible to make the room feel gloomy. Glimmering white walls allowed the pink sofas and vanity chair to really pop with its obnoxious rosy color and ebony woods. A mirror gave me a view of myself and I felt ridiculous with my own fluffy pink dress and tiny golden crown—but there was something else that made me stop and stare.

My eyes.

I scrambled to the mirror and leaned over the vanity to get a better look. Golden specks glimmered in my blue eyes, a color I wasn't used to seeing in my reflection. Malice usually had its hold on me and kept things dark and murky, but now Light poured through me, burning everything in its path and revealing that I was far more infected with Fae magic than I'd realized.

That freaked me out, I'll admit it. I squeezed my eyes shut and searched for my Malice because I really wanted to talk to Zizi right now. I couldn't just let this place take over my body and not even try to fight back. What if it went for my mind next?

That cold familiar wave of dark power was there, but locked in a place inside of my chest so tight that I knew I'd never be able to get to it without some serious damage.

Growling with frustration, I leaned in and glared at my reflection. "I'm not going to let you control me," I told the Light glimmering in my eyes.

It might have been my imagination, but a tinkling giggle sounded through my room.

I glanced at the window to see if the sound had come from outside, but it was securely closed.

Just fabulous. Now my crown is laughing at me.

I WASN'T sure how I was going to get any sleep, but I finally drew the drapes and peeled off my dress, leaving only my underwear and a strap I wore around my chest that Lady Rose had insisted pushed my cleavage up to attractive levels. I'd readjusted it so that it kept my breasts out of the way rather than made them succulent eye candy for fae to feast on, to her great dismay.

There was one piece of princess left to peel off, except, my crown wouldn't allow me to remove it from my head. "I'm going to have to take you off to wash my hair, you know, otherwise I'll look like a flat-haired rat."

The crown seemed to ignore me at first, then pulsed with magic in response, zapping in retaliation before falling off.

"Ouch!" I yelped, but was glad to see the thing had detached itself, yet it made sure I knew this was a temporary parting. A thick tether wrapped around my senses, giving me pressure across my temples that left a subtle desire to put the crown back on. I had a feeling that the compulsion would only grow with intensity over time.

Determined to enjoy my reprieve, I wandered into the washroom and found a massive basin of water with red hot stones lining a basin. A bell labeled "Olivia" glimmered on the wall and I grimaced at it.

I flipped the lever so that the water surged into the bath and steam filled the room. I couldn't think of the last time I'd actually had a *hot* bath, if ever. I was more at home in the cold, but given the Light magic coursing through my veins, a warm bath sounded kind of good right now, so I drew in a deep breath before taking off the last of my underclothes and slipped into the water.

Just when I'd uncovered some oils and started lathering it into my hair, I got the sense that I was no longer alone.

I froze, fingers tangled in the wet strands atop my head, and I scanned the room. The steam made it impossible to see anything.

"Who's there?" I tested. "Olli?"

A shadow moved and I inched lower in the water, slowly slipping to a new location in the large basin. If there was an intruder, I was definitely at a disadvantage, but I wasn't going to be a sitting duck.

"I can smell your fear," a male voice said, making my adrenaline spike. "Were I here to harm you, you'd already be dead by now. I just wanted to talk… in private."

Lucas.

"The folly fae are you doing in my washroom?" I screeched at him and covered myself with my arms, although a thick layer of steam kept both of us obscured from one another. He lingered as a silhouette in the fog, but I could already sense his amusement.

Then his eyes glowed gold, cutting through the steam and fixating on me. "Like I said, I needed to talk to you."

I rolled my eyes and ground my teeth together before responding. "I don't know what kind of manners the fae have, but in the *normal* world barging into someone's bath chambers is considered rude—and creepy."

He hesitated, but I got the sense he was smirking at me. "It's a bit unorthodox, yes, however given your... background, I figured you wouldn't be a prude about it. This is the best way we can talk without anyone knowing. My father doesn't have spies in bath chambers, luckily."

Spies?

Wait... what did he mean by my background?

"Rose Academy isn't a whorehouse," I informed him, desperately hoping he hadn't already figured me out. It was the lesser of two evils if he thought I was a prostitute, and explained our horse ride a bit more.

He chuckled. "Of course. I only meant... never mind that. I came here to tell you that you're not to pass your first class tomorrow."

"Excuse me?"

He cleared his throat as if I hadn't heard him

clearly. "Your first class tomorrow. It would please me if you were not successful in the given task."

I balked at him. "You want me to fail… on purpose?"

He took a step closer, close enough that I could see his fangs as his gaze dipped. I shivered and sank a bit lower into the waters, grateful for the thick white layer of suds and oils that kept most of my body hidden. "That's correct," he said, his words starting to slur around the size of his fangs. "I can see that you have a special relationship with Malice. If my father found out… he'd use you."

Not kill me.

Use me.

That surprised me and I straightened. His eyes widened and I realized now what he'd been looking for. He wasn't trying to cop an eyeful. His gaze fixated on the evidence of my history in the Dregs. My fingers ran over the long, jagged Malice scar that rested over my heart. "If you've already figured me out, then why haven't you told the King?"

His lips lifted in a smile that might have been charming had it not been for the intimidating size of his fangs. Was that a reaction to my Malice… or something else?

"Hey," I snapped, slapping the water to get his attention. "Eyes up here."

He obeyed, his smile growing. "I didn't take you for the shy type," he mused.

I growled. "And I didn't take you for a creep who makes demands while I'm naked. Tell me one good reason why I should fail my classes? I've seen what your father does to those who he deems as 'failures.'"

The memory of the dying girl in my arms made me shiver and fresh rage wafted through my body. Magic, too, tingled across my tongue, and filtered through the water making it glow gold. I could attack the Prince, but I knew better. He was powerful—and fast. He was *fae*. Until I was trained in my new magic or otherwise had access to my Malice again, I wouldn't stand a chance against him.

His nostrils flared as if he could scent my magic and my violent intent. It made his gaze sparkle in a way that made me want to slap him. "I don't have to explain myself to you," he said, amusement and danger dripping from his tone. "I'm the Crown Prince and I've given you an order—which I'm accustomed to being obeyed without question. If you choose insolence, then I'll have to resort to other means to make sure you do not pass your classes. I was only requesting out of courtesy."

"Courtesy?" I shrieked, indignant. "This is hardly a courteous gesture or conversation." I pointed to the door. "Just get out. You're not welcome here."

His eyes flashed with challenge. "As you wish, Crown Princess Candidate. I bid you a pleasant night's rest. You'll need it for tomorrow."

Of course the bastard didn't move towards the door. In a blatant display of power, golden glitter shimmered around him, swirling until he vanished.

Gone.

I hadn't realized the warmth and weighty scent of magic he'd brought to the bath chamber. Without him, the steam settled into lazy wisps and the waters turned tepid. I sank into them and released a long sigh.

"Zizi, I wish you were here," I murmured, and even though the dark pixie didn't materialize or talk to me, a distinct, familiar giggle rang through the room.

Maybe Zizi was gone… but perhaps something else had taken her place.

14

PENNE

*T*he first thing that woke me up was an ache deep in my skull and I groaned, rolling over and tangling myself in bedsheets as I grabbed my head. "Ugh, what is that?"

As if in response, an impatient tapping sounded at my door. "Lady Penelope? Are you awake yet?" Came the worried voice that I recognized as Olli, my handmaiden.

Malice... how did I go from being an all-powerful Malice Caster to a Princess Candidate with a blasted handmaiden?

"Come in," I croaked, then spotted my crown glinting with its own internal golden light on the cushioned chair. I glowered at it.

Olli cracked the door open and peeked inside,

then smiled at me. "You were tired, huh? I don't blame you. The first night I slept in my Princess Room I never wanted to leave." She slipped inside as she spoke and pulled in a cart of supplies.

I sat up, but then grabbed my head again. Fatigue washed over me as if I hadn't slept at all and my Malice scar left a scalding pain against my breast. I pulled the sheets over my breast to hide it from Olli. Luckily she seemed occupied with her cart of crap.

Pain and a faint wave of nausea swept through my body. What the heck was going on with me? My guess was that the Malice and Light magic in my body were definitely not getting along. I would need to figure out something in my classes to better help suppress my Malice, or else I feared how bad this was going to get.

"Lady Penelope?" Olli offered as she held up a bottle of oil and a hairbrush. She gave me a friendly grin. "I imagine your crown is nagging at you to put it back on. I can do your hair first, if you prefer."

I glowered at the crown again, but Olli was right. I'd probably feel better when I put it back on again. "Fine," I grumbled and slipped from the bed and adjusted the pathetic excuse for a nightgown that had been in the dresser, keeping it over my Malice scar. I was so focused on covering my chest that I wasn't paying attention to my surroundings. My nightgown snagged on a corner of the furniture and a rip sounded, making me sigh with frustration. I normally just slept in my leathers just in case I had to make a run for it. I wasn't used to anything so flimsy.

When I faced Olli, I opened my mouth to ask her to hand over the brush. How hard could it be to do my hair? But she was balking at me like I'd grown two heads.

"What is it?" I asked, then realized she was staring at a spot on my left chest.

Oops.

I tugged the nightgown that had slipped thanks to my battle with the furniture, but my efforts did little to cover the scalding mark that ran the full length of my left breast. It was hard enough to hide the thing in the dress the crown had made me wear yesterday. My leathers always covered my body, not to mention my shadows, so I never had to worry about anyone seeing it—at least not until I became a Princess Candidate.

"Is that from orientation?" she asked, her eyes wide.

Sure, that was as good a lie as any. "Yeah," I said, trying to look ashamed. "I think I barely survived

138

that first test. Don't tell anyone about it, okay? I don't think it'll help my chances if the King knew I'd had an… adverse effect."

She pinched her lips and nodded. I didn't trust her, but her fate was linked to mine, so she wasn't going to do anything that would put me in danger… for now. "Of course," she said, giving me a friendly smile. "Secret is safe with me." She slipped around me and placed the oil and brush on the table before grabbing at my hair. "Now, let's get this mess sorted, shall we?"

I endured my first torture session at Olli's hands as she layered the unruly strands with a viciously spiked brush and endless oils, followed by a magical heating device that gave my hair a curl. My head was pounding, both with the compulsion from the crown as well as her ruthless yanks by the time she was done.

"Beautiful!" she exclaimed sometime later, holding up a mirror for me to see her handiwork.

I stared at my reflection. My hair was typically pulled back in a tight bun or tucked underneath a cowl so that it stayed out of my way. Now, though, it unfurled around my shoulders in voluptuous waves. "I didn't even know my hair could do that," I admitted.

Olli brought the mirror closer. "You look beautiful, and you have fae kisses in your eyes! Oh I am so jealous. I never could get mine to come out."

I leaned in to take a better look at the flecks of gold. They reminded me of my Malice scar in the jagged way they tried to take over my features. I decided I didn't like them. "Do you think they'll go away?" I asked. Eventually, I planned on returning to the Dregs. Although, it's not like I had anyone waiting for me there. Jilly would be safe at Rose Academy House and if I stayed in the Kingdom I'd get a chance to see her, even if she didn't need me anymore.

There was Gavin, but I wasn't sure he really counted. Even though he had taken me in, he wasn't exactly a father figure. It was just that I felt at home in the Dregs far more than I did here. I could find more girls like Jilly to help, but not if I had Light in my eyes betraying my connection to the fae.

Maybe I could dissolve the Light in my body when this was all over...

"You want the marks to go away?" Olli asked, her voice going up a pitch as she fluffed my hair for the hundredth time. "I certainly hope not. It's a mark of honor!"

"Right," I grumbled, then winced as my temple

throbbed with a fresh jolt of pain, this one sharper than the last.

Olli tugged my arm. "You can put the crown back on now. Don't make it wait or it's just going to get worse."

I considered seeing how much longer I could resist the crown's compulsion, but decided to pick my battles. I had a feeling that Lucas was going to be getting in my way today and I needed what strength I could muster.

Olli had placed the crown on a little pillow, chiding me that it was not to be stored on the floor. I took the ridiculous, tiny crown and settled it on my head. An instant wave of warmth cascaded through my body and a multitude of aches and pains I had been ignoring vanished.

Olli held out my pink dress, which made me wrinkle my nose. "Doesn't that need to be washed?" I asked. Not that I cared about clothes being washed every day, but I wanted an excuse not to wear the glittering princess outfit.

She grinned and dangled the offending fabric between us. "Oh, don't worry about that. This is a magical garment made by your crown. It can't get dirty."

I rolled my eyes. "Then why couldn't my crown

keep me in perfect hygienic condition?" I could avoid the bath chamber and any uncomfortable future visits from the Crown Prince. I doubted he would visit me while I was on the toilet.

She shrugged. "I suppose it could, but Light magic prefers working on inanimate objects. It's probably worn out just from keeping a compulsion spell on you."

I thumped the piece of metal at my head, hoping I could hurt it. Instead my finger pinged hard against the crown and sent a pleasant tone through the air. "There's a solution to that, you stupid crown. Stop trying to control me and you can have all the magic to yourself."

Olli smirked, but shook her head with disbelief. "I don't believe I've ever met an unwilling Princess Candidate. What were you doing at the Rose Academy House in the first place?" She bit her cheek and waved her hands. "Actually, never mind. Don't answer that. It's better if I don't know too much." She ran to the cart she'd brought in before I question what she meant by that. "I found out that your first class will be Conjuration, so I brought some practice artifacts for you to work with." She beamed with pride as she held up a translucent bauble. "The other maidservants no doubt ever passed that class, but I did and I can tell you right now that practice makes perfect." She held out the orb to me, then laughed and pulled it back. "I suppose I'm getting ahead of myself. You'll have to get dressed first." She put the artifact back with a pile of others. "Would you like help or…?"

I held up the dress and sighed. There were so many buttons and pieces of lace to tie that I wouldn't even know where to start dressing myself in the contraption. "Help, please."

———

AFTER WHAT SEEMED like hours getting into the dress, there was hardly any time left to practice on the artifacts Olli had brought.

"I'm so sorry for not waking you sooner," she lamented, chewing on her lip and glancing at the pile of baubles. "I guess I spent too much time looking for artifacts. I didn't consider how long it would take you to get ready." She glanced at me, betraying that it really *shouldn't* have taken me that long to be presentable.

I rolled my eyes and rubbed my temple that was starting to throb again, although this time it wasn't my crown's fault. "How big of a deal would it have been if I had gone to class in some training leathers?" I offered. Surely I didn't have to go through this ordeal every morning just to look like a proper Princess Candidate.

Olli's eyes went round with shock. "You couldn't possibly leave your chambers without your crown, dress, and hair all in order." I hadn't let her put any paint on my face, and it was the only reprieve she allowed. "Part of your class score will be looking the part, I'm afraid. It's of vital importance."

"Of course it is," I grumbled, then motioned to the door. "All right, well, show me where my class is. I'm sure I'll be fine." I'd been conjuring Zizi all my life without even realizing how smoothly it had come to me. Whatever conjuration exercises they had in mind certainly couldn't be that difficult.

Olli bobbed her head as her eyes glittered with excitement. "That's the spirit. All right, it's just this way, and let me tell you…"

I zoned out as Olli elaborated on all the skills I was going to learn in my classes and how much fun it would be. The way she talked made it clear that she longed to earn her place back in the Academy again, although I couldn't relate. Hatred of the Kingdom and of the Fae was commonplace in the Dregs and I wasn't accustomed to the idea that someone would actually *want* to be a member of Princess Academy—or marry a fae.

"I heard that the Crown Prince will be attending your class," she said, lowering her voice as we approached the classroom.

"Lucas?" I growled under my breath. "Of course. It's not like he has anything better to do than to make my life miserable." I bit my lip from complaining further. Even if Olli was growing on me, I didn't trust her enough to mention that Lucas had paid me a visit or what he'd asked me to do.

She giggled, the sound charming and alluring, almost as if she'd trained all her life for the perfect coy laugh—which, was likely true. "Already on a first name basis? Maybe he'll give you special mentorship." She winked, making me cringe.

"Please. It's not like that."

The Crown Prince was the biggest Malice-wad I'd ever met and the second I learned how to master my powers, he'd be the first fae I was going to teach a lesson.

Olli all but shoved me into the classroom. "I'll be back to pick you up!" she promised before waving and scampering down the long hall. The velvet carpet muffled her steps, but I hadn't expected to feel lonely without her. That unfamiliar feeling

145

crept over me as she disappeared around the corner.

Malice… I was so out of my element here—literally.

Taking a deep breath, I turned and faced the Princess Candidates waiting patiently on stools as ridiculously tiny as their crowns. I smirked at the balancing act for someone in such bulbous gowns to manage to stay up straight.

An older woman brushed my shoulder and gave me a strained smile. "Lady Penelope, I presume? You're right on time. Please, your seat is this way."

It was clear that I was the last one to arrive and being punctual at Crown Princess Academy did not mean being just "on time." The girls whispered behind their hands and I recognized the girl in red who gave me a familiar sultry smirk. The Dregs had taught me not to show weakness and to snuff out superiority before it had time to fester. My fingers flinched, instinct itching for a blade to hold to her throat or Malice to summon around her neck, but a kind warning from my crown reminded me where I was with a flash of heat.

The woman flinched away from me as if my skin had burned her. "Oh dear," she said with a smile. "Your crown must be a feisty one." She gave me another pat on the shoulder as she showed me my excuse for a stool. A tiny pink cushion pinned atop what looked like a painfully weak wooden base. "I'm glad your crown is ready to go. You'll be needing a heavy dose of fae magic for today's lesson."

She cleared her throat and swept to the front of the room. She didn't wear a crown, but her skin suddenly glimmered with golden magic and the girls crooned in response. "I am Lady Rita," she said, her eye glittering with power and fake-friendliness that I knew not to trust. "I graduated Crown Princess Academy ten years ago and have been teaching Conjuration ever since to young hopefuls such as yourselves." Her smile dimmed when she saw I was still standing. "Please take your seat, Candidate Penelope." The sharp tone in her voice said she didn't like giving orders twice.

I regarded the stool again and contemplated the best angle of attack. The other girls were perching on the end as if balanced on the lining of a teacup, so I lowered myself and attempted the same posture, only to teeter over and slap my hands hard against the floor.

"She can't even sit on a Lady's stool!" declared the girl in red and she poorly smothered laughter behind her hand.

"None of that, Candidate Melinda," Lady Rita chided, although she didn't put much effort into it as she flipped through a book on her desk.

"It's because she's from Rose Academy House," whispered a girl in a shimmering indigo dress. She stood out from the others because a small black spade was tattooed just beneath her left eye.

Melinda hummed in agreement, as if that explained everything. She turned her gaze away from me and focused on Lady Rita. "Ignore her, then. I imagine she won't last the day."

If Lady Rita had heard the snide remarks, she didn't chastise the girls further. Instead she pulled out a round bauble from her desk and held it out to us, waiting until I managed to balance on the edge of my pink cushion before speaking. "This, Candidates, is a fae artifact brought from their realm. It is designed to focus Light and allow one with fae magic to target their energies. In our case, we will use this to help us conjure. To conjure is to create matter out of pure magic. It can be a vital tool in fighting Malice." She eyed the windows and curled her shoulders as if someone might hear. "Or perhaps a weapon if you by chance encounter a Dreg-dweller."

The girls gasped and I rolled my eyes.

The door opened, interrupting Lady Rita's speech, and eyes of blue instantly captured my attention.

Lucas.

"Ah, Crown Prince," Lady Rita said with a low curtsey. "You grace us with your presence."

Of course, she didn't fuss at *him* for being *actually* late.

Lucas grinned at me and the ever-present peak of his fangs pointed from his lips. Did the guy have no self-control? Or maybe he just liked to put me on edge. "I hope I haven't missed all the fun. Has anyone conjured something of interest yet?"

"We were just getting started," Lady Rita said and held out the bauble. "I was explaining artifacts—"

Lucas swept past her and, to my horror, pulled up a chair at my side. "Please continue then, Lady Rita. I'll watch from here."

All the girls balked at us, except Melinda who looked like she was about to leap across the classroom and murder me.

"Are you trying to get them to jump me?" I hissed at Lucas.

He chuckled. "No, but you made it clear you weren't going to follow my orders, so I'm here to see that you do as I asked." When I teetered on my stool, threatening to fall again, he placed a hand on my leg to steady me.

If Melinda didn't hate me before, she did now. I was pretty sure she was throwing daggers from her eyes.

I wasn't sure how Lucas planned on making me fail my first day of Conjuration—other than making sure I made enemies of every Princess Candidate in the room —regardless, it was his proximity that put me on edge. His leg grazed mine as he scooted closer and I balanced on the edge of the stool. With the new contact in place, he retracted his grip on my leg. My thighs were already starting to ache trying to stay upright.

"Lean against me," he offered.

I locked my spine, preferring to let my muscles scream rather than accept his assistance.

His warm chuckle sounded again, a throaty masculine sound that made my stomach flip.

I ran one hand up to my crown and tried to adjust it. The magicked metal seeped approving warmth into my head, as if to praise me for winning so much attention from the fae.

Stupid crown.

"Well, let's get started," Lady Rita said, her voice a strangled pitch after seeing how close Lucas was with me. Apparently his behavior was not normal, even for a member of the Queen's Class.

Melinda stood, her movement all grace and elegance that made me hate her guts. "I'd like to try," she said with a sickly-sweet smile towards Lucas and held out a hand.

Lady Rita gave her the bauble. "Focus on the warmth awarded by your crown, dear, and think of any object you'd like most to conjure. Your magic is initially based on instinct, emotions, and—"

Melinda closed her eyes and the artifact glowed with a golden light that heated the room. I went still, waiting to see what Melinda would conjure. A dagger to stab me in the back, perhaps?

When a mystical lantern formed from the threading layers of magic, she opened her eyes and smiled before slipping her fingers through the handle. She held it up, admiring the golden flame inside that continued to spill heat into the room.

Lady Rita clapped her hands and the rest of the girls followed suit, cooing their praise. "Wonderful job, Candidate Melinda!" she exclaimed. "Can anyone tell me what Candidate Melinda just conjured?"

"An icon of the House of Embers," said the girl in

the indigo dress, straightening proudly. "An eternal flame that'll never go out."

"Just like my love for the Crown Prince, should he take me as his bride," she said, winning a smirk from the fae.

Slutty, much?

Lady Rita nodded. "Indeed. I find it no surprise if each of you conjures the icon of your Academy House or family lineage. Fae magic will touch what is most precious to you and bring it to life." She took the bauble back from Melinda and the conjuration dimmed, but held its shape. Melinda frowned at it and furrowed her brows in concentration.

"See how long you can keep it intact, my dear. I will be scoring marks today for the longest conjuration." She brought out her pocketwatch and noted the time. "All right, who's next?"

One by one each girl took her turn. I didn't dare volunteer, not with Lucas's warning presence at my side. Perhaps he thought to make me fail by having me suffer the boredom of this class.

To pass the time I tried to memorize each girl's name and match it with her face as Lady Rita made her rounds. Life in the Dregs taught me to remember a face, but I wasn't so good with names. The girl in indigo was Julia from the House of

Spades—naturally, to match the tattoo below her left eye. It was no surprise that she summoned the playing card that marked her house, apparently it was a representation of fortune and nobility among the Elites. She had the haughty attitude for it—that was for sure.

The other girls conjured their objects without fail, of which I was glad. Perhaps that meant no one would be dying today. Although it also meant I had more competition and I needed to learn these girls, their quirks, motivations, and their angle. I was hopeless at remembering all of their names so I separated them by their dresses in yellow, green, purple, and blue. I made a mental note to watch the girl in blue named Rylie. She was the only one who conjured something interesting, a small flute that she began to play with a haunting melody.

"Seems like it's Pink's turn," Melinda barked over the music, cutting Rylie off.

The girl in blue frowned and lowered her instrument and gave me a glance. She was the only one who didn't have hatred in her eyes—but she did have a deep melancholy aura that clung to her and had been so beautifully expressed by her music. "If the Crown Prince permits," she offered, having taken note that Lucas refused to leave my side.

Lucas cleared his throat and reluctantly eased away from me, leaving me colder than I was a moment before. "Of course."

Melinda snatched the artifact from Rylie's grasp and held it out to me. "Well come on, *Pink*, let's see if you can conjure a rose. You can do that, right? Seems easy enough."

I didn't know what I would conjure, but it definitely wouldn't be a rose marked from the lowly Academy House. If magic really worked off instinct, I had the full intention of conjuring a weapon, which I would promptly stab in Melinda's eye socket.

When I attempted to stand from my precarious position on the stool, a zap of pain struck through my temple and I winced. It was the same sensation I'd felt the day before when Lucas had been doing *something* to get me to shut up when talking to his father.

This time, the pain wasn't a warning, but a deliberate act to put me off balance—not that it was hard to do.

Lucas's hand shot out as if to steady me, but his grip slipped under the loop of my sleeve and he gripped my shoulder harder than necessary to keep me from falling. He jabbed his thumb strategically over my Malice scar and scalding heat scorched through me like a thousand flaming knives.

I didn't cry out. I was used to pain, as it was how I fueled my Malice, but it was exactly the kind of sensation that sent my darker powers to life.

"Careful," he said with a light smirk tugging his handsome lips. A deep cold yearning to slam him into the wall nearly overtook all my senses.

It was Melinda who broke my attention on the Crown Prince and shoved the artifact in my face. I took it and hissed at the pain as the artifact enhanced the Light surging from my crown that was already trying to attack my Malice.

"Go on, conjure something," she sniped, crossing her arms and giving me a *I-dare-you* look, as if she wouldn't believe me capable of conjuration until she saw it with her own two eyes.

I gripped onto the bauble even harder, trying to talk to my crown in my head at the same time.

Will you focus, stupid crown? The Malice is not the problem. You're the problem! I need to conjure something —preferably a weapon I can use against both the Crown Prince and the brat in the red dress.

My crown ignored me, fully invested in surging my body with golden magic to offset the Malice that Lucas had sent reeling through my body.

"Dear, you're using the Light but you're over-whelming the artifact. You must focus," Lady Rita instructed, although I sensed the note of worry in her voice. After ten years as a professor at the Academy, she should be able to see something wasn't quite right with me.

I ground my teeth before replying. "I just... need a minute."

The girl in the indigo dress barked a haughty laugh. "Well *all* of us conjured our object the moment we touched the artifact." She glared at Lady Rita. "Doesn't seem fair to give her extra time, now does it?"

"I'm afraid you're right, Candidate Julia," Lady Rita solemnly agreed and held out her hand. "The artifact, please."

My stomach clenched as I held onto the bauble, desperately trying to get my wild magic under control. Light billowed through me like a storm, chomping at the bit to devour the Malice that Lucas had brought to life. It wasn't natural for me to suppress the icy shadow. I wanted to embrace it, but the harder I tried to revert to the person I'd been in the Dregs, the more the tiny crown atop my head reminded me how much I'd changed overnight.

I was a Crown Princess Candidate, dress, crown, douchebag prince and all.

My Light floundered when Melinda wrenched the artifact from my grip and handed it over to Lady Rita. "She looked like she was about to pass out," she offered with a delicate shrug.

Lady Rita sighed and returned the bauble to her drawer. "I'm afraid I have to give you failing marks for today, Lady Penelope."

"And what does that mean?" I snapped, every nerve ending feeling like it was on fire. I whirled on Lucas. "What happens when I fail a class?"

He shrugged. "Nothing you can't handle, I'm sure."

Of course he was going to be useless, as well as obnoxious.

Lady Rita clapped her hands. "All right, everyone. Show me your conjurations. I still must award your points for today."

Melinda proudly held up her lantern that was glowing just as brightly as when she'd first conjured it. Although, she'd touched the artifact just now, so she could have conjured it twice without anyone noticing. "Mine is still as good as new," she said with a smug smirk, her crown glinting with the firelight

157

from her lantern as she glanced at me with a sense of victory.

I rolled my eyes. Yeah, she definitely cheated.

The rest of the girls showed what was left of their conjurations. Rylie's flute had wilted, followed by the girls in yellow, green, and purple dresses having lost their conjurations altogether. Lady Rita awarded everyone golden slips sized according to their score —I, of course, didn't get anything.

"Present your slips at lunch." She instructed with a formal scowl, which I assumed was her serious face. She pointedly avoided my gaze as she waved to the door. "Please proceed to the dining hall just down and to your right. Further instruction will await you there, as well as your maidservants to accompany you."

"Will you be joining us, Your Highness?" Melinda asked Lucas with an innocent batting of her eyelashes. I wanted to gag.

Lucas watched me as I struggled to adjust my dress out from under my feet so I could follow the rest of the girls out the door. The only small comfort I got from his attention was that it enraged Melinda to no end. "I have other matters to attend to," he said, not taking his gaze off of me. "But I'll be keeping an eye on the Queen's Class."

His silver eyes sparkled with delight. He'd won—today's battle, at least.

I managed to manhandle my dress and ignored them both as I made slow progress, clicking my way to the door.

How did these girls walk in such ridiculous shoes? I hated being a Princess Candidate, and I imagined my trials had only just begun.

15

PENNE

Where the heck was the Crown Prince going that was more important than making my life miserable?

Right, didn't care.

Free from the classroom, I was met with another audience that judged my every movement. At first I thought them Elites, based on their silken dresses. Yet, when I did a double-take and spotted Olli among them, I realized these were handmaidens.

I almost didn't recognize Olli right away. She looked more like Lady Olivia than someone who was supposed to serve me. Her brown hair bounced in fashionable curls pinned securely to the side of her face and a low, sleek dress showed off her cleavage, but in a fashionable way. I noticed a pink rose pin on her left sleeve that glittered with innate magic, marking her as my servant. I wonder what other properties it had that Lucas hadn't told me about. He'd mentioned that his father had spies. In a world of magic, anything could be a listening device. Was that pin one of his ways that he listened in on conversations? I needed to be careful.

Olli gave me a trained smile and parted from the other handmaidens. "How did it go?" she began, then glanced down at my empty hands and frowned. "Where's your slip?"

I gathered up my dress in my fists, yanking it nearly to my knees so that I could storm around her. "Didn't get one, okay? Let's go to this stupid lunch."

The other handmaidens gasped at my behavior and Olli hurried to my side, tugging the folds of my dress down to less unseemly levels. "That's impossible. I know we didn't get to practice, but I can feel your Light magic from here. It's absolutely pouring off of you." She wafted her hands around me, fanning away the golden mist I was exuding. "And stop handling your dress like it's a sack of potatoes. You'll get negative marks for propriety if one of the professors sees you."

I snorted, which I'm sure added to the unladylike appearance I was purposefully going for. "Then let them give me negative marks." It would probably just speed along whatever plans Lucas had for me, the bastard. To accentuate my point, I ripped off my shoes and made my way down the hall as Olli gasped at me. "Relax," I snapped, "I'll put them back on before we get there."

"You don't understand," Olli said, keeping her voice low as she made a strained effort to keep up with me. "There are consequences for failure or disobedience." She let out a long breath. "You'll see what I mean at lunch."

I didn't like the edge of fear in her voice.

We stepped off the velvet carpet and crossed an opal walkway, making Olli's tiny shoes click against the surface in a frenzy as she tried to match my pace. I would have admired how even a floor could be beautiful and sparkled with its own inner light had I not known the cost of such finery. If Malice worked off of pain and suffering, I wondered how the fae got their Light magic. By the experiences I'd had so far, it wasn't through happiness or joy, like Jilly might have suggested. She always tried to see the best in things.

I rather imagined that fae got their power from sacrifice, just like Malice, only theirs was a slow seduction of power. I had to be careful how much control I gave the Light over my body.

First to arrive at the long dining table, I put on my shoes and found my chair with its pink cushion ready and waiting for me. I wanted to get this day over with, so I marched over to it, ignoring the butler who tried to hurry and pull it out for me. Instead, I yanked the chair and sat myself down and gave him a glare until he bowed and backed away.

The head of the table was empty and I wondered if the King would be joining us again.

Olli pulled up a small stool at my side, slightly behind me. Guess she wasn't allowed to eat. When still no one arrived, I peered over my shoulder at her. "I doubt the others were in such a hurry to get here." She pointed at my shoes.

Right. I snatched up a napkin and threaded it through my fingers. "So, have any news of the outside world? Might as well chat while we wait."

She smiled, surprising me. "I heard that there was a disturbance on the border," she offered, her words impressively low so that I could just barely hear her. "Heard some of the guards talking about it."

I decided that Olli would make a good spy if I ever had the pleasure of destroying this place and needed a few allies in the Kingdom.

"What kind of disturbance?" I asked.

She writhed her hands. "Malice, of course. What else would be important enough to warrant the King *and* Crown Prince's attention?"

So, that's where Lucas had scurried off to. A fleeting curiosity made me wonder if he'd delayed his departure in order to attend my class—and ensure my first grade was a big fat zero. Glad to see I was so important to him.

Rolling my eyes, I turned my attention back to the dining table. If there was Malice invading the Kingdom again, I should be out there making sure Jilly was safe. I would definitely check on her the second I figured out how to cross the forest on my own, or at least get word back to her. Surely the Academy allowed some sort of outside communication—and if they didn't, I would figure out a way.

The other girls filtered in and took their seats. Melinda settled in to my right and a girl in yellow to my left. I tried casting my gaze across the table, only to find the girl with the spade tattoo glaring at me, a girl in purple pretending to be fascinated with her lap, and Rylie, the girl in blue, who gave me a light nod of recognition.

This is going to be a long day.

The entrance door to the dining hall slammed

shut and we all flinched, regarding the new arrival with wide eyes.

A fae—one far more sinister and beautiful than the King—grinned at us, showing off his pointed fangs. Fine creases from his eyes betrayed his years and his pointed ears had a slight curl to them. Fae seemed to age well, so my guess was this one was practically ancient. "Hello, Candidates," he all but purred. "I'm afraid the King and his son are otherwise occupied and they send their apologies. I will be overseeing today's score results for the Queen's Class." He gave a light bow of his head, his silver hair tumbling over his shoulders with the motion. The girls followed suit, bowing their heads in respect. I, of course, stared dumbly and wondered why no one had cared to tell me there'd be more fae wandering around the Academy.

Olivia pinched my elbow. "That's Surin, the Light instruction professor."

Coming to my senses, I stared at my hands in my lap. It made sense that a fae would teach their own magic at the Academy, and if anyone could help me learn how to get a handle on the Light my crown forced on me, it would be another fae.

But I can't trust anyone.

Only Lucas, and Olli by accident, knew about my

Malice scar but I didn't see him jumping to my rescue anytime soon.

Guess I was just going to have to get creative.

With a new goal in mind, I let my rage wash out of me and replaced it with purpose. That's how I'd survived the Dregs for so long, not by wallowing in my emotions, but focusing myself in control.

Professor Surin adjusted his suit, which was an attractive silver that contrasted against the gold motes dancing around him. He had Light—and a lot of it. It moved with him as naturally as he glided through the room. It was hard not to admire him, but I would keep my distance for now. This was still a fae.

A human butler pulled out his chair and bowed as the fae took the King's seat. He nodded his thanks to the servant, which already said volumes about him and made me want to trust him in spite of myself.

I would have preferred to watch the fae from a distance, learn his patterns, and figure him out before making my first impression. Yet I didn't have any shadows to slip into here and I was on full display, pink dress and all. Reconnaissance was not an option.

Professor Surin glanced down at the list by his

plate that had each of our names associated with the color of our dresses. My stomach clenched when I noted that one had been crossed out.

The fae gave me a smile, which I guessed was supposed to be friendly in spite of the sinister fangs poking from his lips. "Candidate Penelope, I presume?"

I gave him a polite nod, although it probably looked more like I'd had a mini-seizure. I wasn't used to this Princess Candidate thing. "That's correct."

He glanced at the golden slips neatly placed on empty plates in front of each girl—and then looked again to my empty platter. "I see that you haven't earned a slip today. I suppose I'll get a front row seat to just how powerful your Light is." He grinned. "By what I can see, you have enough Light to survive. I wouldn't worry."

Was that supposed to be encouraging?

I gave Olli a quick backward glance, but she shook her head. Whatever was going down was something I was going to have to deal with on my own.

A collection of servants came in with tiny silver platters, each with a champagne glass filled with a black drink. I recognized the familiar cool shadows that spoke of secrets and empty promises, filling the room with ominous whispers.

They weren't even trying to hide it this time, and by the swirling shadows that puffed over the rims, this was a much stronger dose.

Many of the girls gasped, but Melinda straightened and ran a finger over her oversized ticket on her plate. She flashed me a smug grin.

"You've been given your first scores," Professor Surin began, "which means your reward is a dilution of the Malice." He picked up Melinda's slip and admired it. "The better your score, the larger your slip, and the more Light at your disposal during this trial." He placed the slip back down. "However, even with top marks there is a small dose that you must disperse on your own. And for those of you with few marks, or no marks at all," he glanced at me and at my empty platter again, "you must prove yourself worthy to remain a member of the Queen's Class by dispersing the Malice without any assistance."

Rylie only had a small ticket and paled when the servant placed her drink in front of her.

"What if we don't drink it?" I suggested, not for myself, but for Rylie. She seemed sweet, but the look on her face said she didn't think she was going to survive this round. No one deserved to die just to appease the fae. "We've only been here a day. What kind of test is this that there's no room for preparation or leeway?"

"Leeway?" Melinda snapped, overriding the fae who'd opened his mouth to reply. "Don't be sore just because you couldn't conjure a simple object. You must do your duty as a Princess Candidate." She glanced down at her platter and gathered her ticket, plunking it into the drink. The golden strip sizzled and evaporated, thinning the murky drink with golden glitter until it was nearly clear. She held it aloft and grinned. "May the best become the Crown Princess to protect the Kingdom." She knocked back the drink, emptying it in four strong gulps.

"I'm afraid Candidate Melinda has a point, even if she lacks elegance in her response," Professor Surin said to me, grinning when Melinda widened her eyes at the insult.

"My apologies, Professor," Melinda said, putting the empty flute down. She folded her hands in her lap and bowed her head. "I did not mean to speak out of turn."

"Of course," he offered, although it didn't sound sincere. He turned his attention to me, his eyes crinkling around the edges in a way that made him look almost friendly. "To answer your question, if you do not drink the Malice in front of you, then you will be forced." The butlers at his back stiffened as if waiting for the order to pin me down and cram Malice down my throat. The fae gave me a flat stare. "I would recommend cooperation, however you are free to make your own choices." He turned his attention to the rest of the table. "All of you must choose; choose for yourself, or choose for the Kingdom. The graduates of Crown Princess Academy are the only forces standing between the all-consuming Malice and the last haven humanity has to offer. As fae, we are here to supply our magic, but it is you who must wield it."

That clicked something inside of my brain...

The fae couldn't fight Malice.

That explained why the Academy had been founded in the first place, and also confirmed my suspicions that the fae had something to do with Malice being unleashed on our world.

They needed us.

Because someone wanted them dead.

Too bad the fae had figured out a way to use the human realm as a shield.

I curled my fingers around my glass, recognizing the dull cold that sank into my bones on contact. I wasn't looking forward to reliving the prior day's experience. It had taken some serious convincing to get my crown to allow the Malice to hole up in my scar instead of being destroyed. I couldn't just "disperse" Malice like Melinda was doing now, showing off her power as tiny black lines spidered across her arms only to be expelled in a flash of gold. She gave me a triumphant smirk, as if the tiny bit of Malice she'd dispersed was some great feat that I'd never be able to accomplish.

Maybe she was right.

In the Dregs, I was the most powerful Malice Caster in existence. But here… here I was on unfamiliar ground.

I wasn't cut out to be a Crown Princess Candidate. My crown had chosen me by accident, surely. A fae had taken it to the Dregs and the poor crown must have gotten confused, no doubt. For all I knew, that fae could have been Lucas himself. I hadn't stopped until now to really consider that, or what it meant. Why would Lucas bring the crown to the Dregs?

Rylie was the first to take up her glass. Her blue eyes that matched her dress flashed to meet mine. Even though her hand shook and the Malice inside of the delicate flute threatened to slosh over the side, I thought Rylie was the bravest person I'd ever met. I decided then and there that I wouldn't let anything happen to her. I wasn't going to watch another girl die in this wretched place.

She plunked in her ticket and waited for the Malice to fade, although it didn't react nearly as much as Melinda's had. She sighed at it with resignation and then took a gentle sip, grimacing.

"Just drink it," Melinda scoffed impatiently. "It's not going to drink itself." At her glower, the other girls placed their tickets into their glasses and waited for the golden bubbles to calm before bringing the Malice to their lips.

I took mine, void of any golden refinement, and frowned. Olli gave my shoulder a light squeeze.

"Here it goes, then," I said, then downed it, knocking the drink back like Melinda had done and held on for dear life when the icy-cold burn came.

THIS WAS DEFINITELY A STRONGER dose than orientation. My crown immediately reacted, flooding my senses with Light. Instead of helping matters, Light and Malice clashed in my body, sending a thousand tiny icy daggers through my system.

Gritting my teeth, I screamed in my head at the unrelenting magic.

Don't try to destroy it or you're going to kill me!

This time, my blasted crown seemed to listen and pulled back just enough that I could gulp in a fresh breath of air. The cold serrated sensations moved to my extremities and I looked down to see if my skin was splitting open, but only the recognizable black streaks clawed their way under my skin. It wouldn't damage me, not if I accepted the Malice like I always had. In fact, I could sense the underlying current of power that begged to be used. All Malice wanted was a purpose and a place, just like anyone else lost in this world, and it was because of that kindred suffering I had with Malice that I'd always known how to communicate with it.

You're home, I told it, hoping that my inner voice could still reach the darkness that streaked through me in panicked desperation. It wasn't trying to hurt me, but trying to claim a place of its own. Malice was naked and vulnerable in the world and if allowed a chance, it could become an ally.

It just needed the right host.

I'd always been more than capable of that role.

The scar above my heart accepted the Malice as it found its way through my system. Relief made me let out the breath I'd been holding. My crown sizzled atop my head, making a big show of it, but it seemed to be for the spectators' benefit. Everyone was staring at me, the most interested being Surin who watched with a calculated gaze as I "dispersed" the Malice.

"Impressive, Candidate Penelope," he praised.

Melinda *humphed*, as if she hoped I'd fall over dead, and accepted a fresh glass of sparkling orange juice from a butler. She leisurely sipped at it as she watched me down the ridge of her nose.

The other girls had sweat lining their brows, but were otherwise going to survive—except maybe Rylie. She clutched her stomach and heaved over the table, black streaks leaving raised bruises across her skin. Her bloodshot eyes snapped open wide as she stared directly at me, seeming to plead with me to save her.

That was all the encouragement I needed.

Bunching up my dress, I leapt over the table amidst the cascade of gasps and kicked my way to Rylie, careless of the expensive tableware I was trampling.

"Blessed fae!" Melinda shouted, flinging her arms over her head. "Somebody do something! She's gone feral!"

Ignoring her, I dove for Rylie. Her lips turned blue and darkness invaded her eyes, taking over the color of her irises as she clawed at her throat. The Malice was overwhelming her, suffocating her, and I didn't have much time left.

I wasn't going to try and suck the Malice out of her like I'd failed with the last girl. I needed to change my tactic. Malice and I didn't get along right now, but something Olli had said gave me an idea.

Thanks to Lucas, I had a surplus of Light magic that I didn't know what to do with. I couldn't destroy Malice… not my own Malice, anyway. But what about Malice that wasn't in my body? Perhaps it would be sated with Rylie as an outlet.

Directing the heat from my crown through my fingers, I gripped Rylie by the shoulders and focused. "Hold still," I whispered, hating the mewling sounds coming from her as she tried to obey.

Light exuded from me in waves that mimicked my heartbeat, thundering through my ears and gnawing at the edges of my senses looking for something to devour, to burn, to destroy. Light was so much more vicious than Malice. I'd never realized just how powerful or how hungry it would be.

The Light wanted to go after the closest source: The Malice in my chest, but I fought it and pushed it through my fingertips. Not much of it would obey me, but it was enough to clear the Malice from Rylie's eyes.

I could have done more, but strong hands ripped me away from the girl and I shrieked at the blazing heat that scalded my skin.

Surin slammed me against the wall and growled, his fangs extended in warning and his eyes ablaze with white heat. "Enough of that," he said, his words having an ebb and flow to them that made the whole world seem ethereal.

Surin was powerful in the Light, far more skilled than I and made me feel that I'd done something very, very wrong.

"Everyone to your chambers. Today's session is done. You've lived to see another day at the Academy." The other girls stared until Surin flashed his gaze at them, sending Light streaking across the room. "I said out!"

With squeaks of compliance, the girls scooted out of their seats and hurried to the door, keeping their heads ducked as they shuffled past us.

The butlers—who were really just fancy guards— kept to their posts with hands clasped behind their back and eyes forward. I assumed they were waiting for a command and otherwise would stay in place like the good little statues they were.

Rylie gasped for breath as she clutched onto the dining table for support. Black still marred her veins, but she was breathing. She gulped in another breath as her eyes cleared of shadow. She was going to survive.

Surin lifted his lip in a snarl at me. "Tell me what artifact you drained, Candidate, or I'll give you negative marks." His eyes widened, making me squint as the brilliance of his magic hit my face.

I blinked at him. "I don't know what you're talking about."

He closed in on my personal space, the heat of his magic making me sweat. Surin was a powerful fae, one to be feared and respected. I got the sense that he wasn't used to repeating himself as his golden eyes bore into mine. "No one has that much Light at their disposal—no human, anyway. You downed an entire flute of Malice. It should have been enough to make you go unconscious, but what do you do? You leap across the table and throw your Light around like it's a toy." He gripped my arm, making me wince as the scalding heat sliced through my senses. "Who are you?"

My mouth bobbed open and closed, unable to

come up with a suitable lie. "I didn't have any time to practice," I blurted. "Olli brought me some artifacts before class, but I swear I didn't have time to do anything."

He narrowed his eyes. "Lady Olivia always was a troublemaker."

I didn't want to throw Olli under the horse carriage, but that was a better excuse than this fae realizing that something was off about me. "She meant to help me," I insisted, hoping to keep him focused on Olli instead of what might be off about me. "You can go check my room for yourself. Olli didn't break any rules." I hoped that was true. I doubted Olli would really be stupid enough to piss off the fae.

He studied me for a long time, making me endure the heat of his magic before he relented and released me. "I'll have a guard verify your story." He snapped his fingers and one of the butlers moved from his post, sprinting through the doorway before I had a chance to blink.

Professor Surin turned to Rylie as his magic died down to less blazing levels. A golden mist followed him as he moved. He clasped his hands behind his back and glanced down at her while she was still on the floor. "It seems you've survived," he said flatly, "although it's unprecedented to have another Candidate's support." He clicked his tongue. "I'll have to discuss with the King how to proceed."

I resisted the urge to roll my eyes. I couldn't imagine that would go over very well. "No one said there were any rules about not supporting one another," I protested. "What if we were out in the field and this was a Malice breach? Wouldn't it be to the benefit of the Kingdom if we could save one another instead of letting Malice pick us off one by one?"

The silver streak of Surin's brow raised as he regarded me. "Light has always been treated as a self-centered magic. What you pulled off today was… unique. But, if it could be replicated, perhaps your proposal has merit." He adjusted one of his cuffs. "I'll be sure to include your proposal with my report. New ideas are useful, after all." He turned and took a few steps towards the door, then paused. "Useful, if you survive to graduation, that is. Do be careful with your abilities, Candidate Penelope, as well as your choice in allies." He hesitated, as if debating to say more, then nodded and left the room, leaving me alone with a handful of statuesque guards dressed as butlers and Rylie who was starting to look pale, although I doubted that was due to her exposure to Malice.

Brushing myself off, I sighed and marched over to her and offered her a hand. "Are you ready to get out of here?"

She swallowed, then slipped her fingers into mine. "Absolutely."

LUCAS

*T*he last place I wanted to be was by my father's side trekking through the evacuated edges of the Kingdom, especially when Penelope was undergoing her first real dose of Malice. The tiny sliver she'd had at initiation would be nothing compared to today's dose and I wanted to see how she would handle it. I had no doubt that she'd survive, although a niggling in the back of my mind made me feel guilty.

It would hurt—a lot.

As a fae I couldn't disperse Malice myself, but I could relocate it, or even block it, that went for Light as well. Penelope was special. She didn't even realize how special she was. She almost had a relationship with Malice, and she was building one with her

Light as well. Given time, she would be capable of unprecedented things.

Things that would achieve what I could not.

End the fae.

But to build her skills, I had to make sure she digested Malice at each trial and learned how to control her Light. It didn't give me any pleasure that I had the unique ability to antagonize both the Malice and Light in her, but this was how I was going to break the cycle. She was the key to everything.

"Seal off the perimeter," my father barked, sending three guards to hurry down the streets with blades drawn, as if that was really necessary.

The long barrier of glimmering opal magic between the Kingdom and the Dregs kept the wave of angry Malice at bay, although I could spot the cracks starting to form.

"Why didn't we bring graduates with us?" I sniped, trying not to get worried that this entire segment was about to give way to the heavy Malice on the other side. "We need to disperse the Malice before we reinforce this barrier." I was stating the obvious, but my father hadn't brought anyone with the power to extinguish Malice.

"Most of them are in the Fae Realm dealing with

more important matters," he said absently as he stormed down the barrier. He kept his distance from the crackling energy that neither of us could fight. Malice was our weakness and our only defense was to push it back. "We're here to keep the Malice from spreading any further into the Kingdom, not to waste precious resources dispersing it."

Of course. What else would be a better waste of time than witnessing destruction and doing nothing about it?

"There's Malice leaking into the Kingdom," I reiterated, hoping my father could see how ridiculous he was being. Even if we sealed off the breach, we'd still be leaving Malice inside the barrier.

He took a long look at the whitewashed walls of evacuated mansions. The only color that flashed across them was the red warning lights of fae magic. Tiny motes burst in little explosions when in close proximity of Malice, ruining the otherwise lovely ambiance of the property. This place had been home to Elites, perhaps the less wealthy Elites to live so close to the Dregs, but Elites nonetheless. Everything was spotless with clean, glistening windows and the insides sparkling with luxurious long-armed sofas and dining tables that had been left behind the moment the alert had activated.

Across the ground, the span of stone and grass abruptly ended at the border where the Dregs waited on the other side. I realized with a sharp intake of breath that not everyone had evacuated in time—which made sense. The Dregs didn't have advanced alert systems in place to let them know when the dark substance was overtaking yet more ground and until the breach, they wouldn't have been able to see directly into Elite territory where the alarms blared with panic.

They were trapped. Skinny, raggedy women clung to one another with their eyes locked on the shadows licking at their feet. The men had already died trying to get out, their corpses lost in the murky depths.

I took a step forward, instinct telling me to save those stranded above a rising tide of Malice, but my father's stern gaze made me stop in my tracks.

"You pity them," he said—a statement.

My father didn't know me very well, but he'd read me way too quickly. I could have smacked myself for revealing that I cared about humans. Although there wasn't anything I could do for them without an Academy graduate here to disperse the Malice, but it felt impossible to just let them wither and die.

I sneered at him, doing my best to look pissed off. "I value resources," I retorted, to which he instantly relaxed.

"Ah, yes," he said, a note of approval in his tone. "Humanity does grow scarce these days. It is a pity that we can't salvage their potential in full, but I assure you, the Kingdom system we've put in place is sufficient and self-sustaining." He frowned, then approached a small crack in the barrier that I'd missed. He hovered his hand over it, pooling his magic to push the Malice back and seal the barrier. "Find where Malice has breached the Kingdom and seal it off. This will have to do for now." When I didn't respond, he broke his concentration long enough to glare at me. "If you wish to salvage resources, you have to protect what is yours, first. Trust me, son. The Kingdom is fragile if not properly maintained, so do your part. If you find a queen strong enough, perhaps you can even expand the Kingdom, but for now…" His words trailed off as he turned his attention back to his work, Light billowing from him and sending the Malice screeching back into the Dregs where it floundered before pushing the tide higher and threatening the stragglers.

This was menial work, but only the royal line still

had magic. Humans didn't know that, so it explained my father's efforts to make sure we weren't spotted for this task. We'd come well after all the Elites had evacuated and my father wore simple robes, far less extravagant than his usual attire.

A baby's cry broke me from my musings, springing me back to reality. One of the women had a child. *A child.* It wasn't fair. I couldn't just stand by while the innocent and helpless were devoured by Malice.

Without thinking, I inched around my father and shoved my hand through one of the larger cracks, sending light blasting a path through the Malice. It wouldn't last very long, but it would be long enough.

The women screeched and blinked at me, their dull eyes glassy with loss, but I growled at them, showing my fangs. It was enough of a jolt that they startled to their feet and took the path I'd made for them to safety. The woman with a baby was the only one who seemed to realize I'd been aiming to help them and gave me a wary smile before clutching the baby to her chest and disappeared down the break in Malice before it reclaimed the ground.

An ache in my chest formed where I'd overexerted myself, but the sight of the few humans I'd been able to save gave that hollow space where my mother used to be a sense of warmth I hadn't felt in a long time.

"Stubborn boy," said my father, and whether he knew my true motivations or not, I didn't care.

At least I'd saved a few.

17

PENNE

"How is such a tiny thing so heavy?" I griped, complaining about Rylie's weight pulling on my already sore shoulders as I dragged her back to her room.

Rylie wasn't the type to accept help, which I could tell by the firm set of her jaw, but she didn't have a say in the matter this time. I wasn't going to let the fae keep getting away with this.

"You could just leave me," she offered, her tone unamused but a spark in her eyes saying that she was grateful.

"And get negative marks for littering? No thanks."

That won me a smirk.

Olli trailed behind us as we bantered, fretting the

whole way. Rylie's own maidservant was so fed up with the whole thing that she'd abandoned us completely.

"I'd invite you in, but I don't want to get you into more trouble," Rylie croaked.

"Nonsense," I said and thrust open her door, revealing a room adorned with every shade of blue imaginable. A wall filled with various small fluted instruments glittered against the fading sunlight that spilled in from a cracked window. "Wow."

She chuckled. "If you're impressed with my room, you should see Melinda's."

I shuddered. "No thanks."

Hauling Rylie inside, I gave Olli a glare. "You going to help or are you just going to stand there?"

Olli chewed on her lip, contemplating for a moment before she sighed and followed me into Rylie's room. "She's right, you know. You could get in trouble for being here. We really should get back—"

"There are guards stripping my pink excuse for a room as we speak, right? Do you really want to walk in on that right now?" I snapped.

Olli winced. "No, I guess not."

"So pissing off the fae is today's goal?" Rylie asked. "Professor Surin would likely expect you to be reprimanded in your quarters. Wouldn't be surprised if he showed up himself later for the task."

I snorted. "Then I definitely don't want to go back to my room. Pissing off the fae is definitely today's goal."

Rylie perked up as I settled her onto the plump edge of her bed. "You could stay here, if you mean that." She glanced around the room. Everything was pristine and untouched. "I haven't really used it, to be honest. I prefer the Music Hall." She wobbled, threatening to tumble over.

Gently pushing her down onto the bed, I pulled the blanket over her. She couldn't have been very comfortable in her dress, but I wasn't about to disturb her as she fluttered her eyes closed. "Tell me about the Music Hall," I suggested.

She yawned and a glimmer of gold trickled through her veins and shone through her skin. I realized there were still traces of Malice being eliminated in her body, the poor thing. She wasn't like me —well, very few people were like me.

"I'll do better," she murmured, rolling on her side and tucking the blanket under her chin. "I'll show you tomorrow and give you a lesson. Music is one of our classes, so consider it repayment." Without opening her eyes she reached out and squeezed my hand. "Not sure where you came from, but it sure wasn't Rose Academy House." When I flinched, she chuckled, cracking one eye open. "Your secret is safe with me."

I SHOULD HAVE HATED myself that one of the Candidates had already figured out that I was an impostor. Instead, I had a strange sense of relief that I carried with me all through that night and well into the next day.

In spite of being in another Candidate's chamber, I was forced into my obligatory bath in the morning, thanks to Olli's insistence that I not earn any negative marks over something as simple as hygiene. Water, like most resources, was a precious commodity in the Dregs and a bath was simply a luxury we did not have. Lakes or ponds were soon contaminated with Malice and it was dangerous to spend any sort of time near large bodies of water. Finding enough pure water to carry into homes, much less heating it, was a rare pleasure.

Of course, I should have known better than to get comfortable. The moment I slipped into the steaming waters and let out a sigh, I felt that sensation of being *watched.*

"You really have to stop creeping up on me like this," I grumbled without opening my eyes.

A male chuckle caressed me through the murky vapors of lavender and blossom and heat. It was a rather seductive setting, which might work in my favor, so I decided to go with it and rested my head back against the porcelain edge. I felt his eyes on me —Lucas, a dangerous fae I had no business taunting, but it was hard to resist when he made it so easy.

"I needed to talk with you... privately," he said, his low voice making my toes curl in spite of myself.

"That excuse again?" I murmured, slipping my fingers through the water and trailing droplets over my chest. I wasn't sure how close he was, but I didn't feel like I was in danger. There was something that Lucas needed from me and until he got it, I had the power in our interactions. "If you wanted to see me naked then you should be fae enough to admit it. Isn't your race supposed to be shameless?"

He coughed and I peeked one eye open to see his averted gaze. Had I embarrassed him?

Odd, not what I expected from someone like the Crown Prince who probably had a new girl every night—at least, that's what I expected from a gorgeous fae in power. Perhaps I'd misjudged him.

"I'm here to tell you that my father has returned to the Fae Realm," he said, his words all business. "The guards will be watching you for the next couple of days, but there will be a period where they lax their watch when my father returns. It'll be the only chance you can get out of the Academy."

My eyes went wide. "Leave the Academy?"

He nodded. "Malice has breached the Kingdom. For some reason my father and all of the Academy graduates are in the Fae Realm right now, so there's no one to disperse it."

I scoffed and sank deeper into the warm waters. "I'm supposed to care about some Elites?"

Lucas took a daring step closer, his gaze locked on me in a way that made a chill run up my spine. I was still covered enough from the steam and murky water frothed with oils, but if I shifted at all…

"That section of the Kingdom has been evacuated, but the Dregs weren't so lucky."

I stiffened. "Since when do you care about the Dregs?"

"Always," he said without hesitation. "Perhaps a bit more than I should since I met you."

If that statement had intended to make me slip

out of the safety of the murky waters, it worked. I jolted upright, forgetting that I was completely naked.

Lucas's gaze dipped, his fangs elongating before he turned from me. "Perhaps you should cover yourself with a towel," he suggested, his words slurring as he tried to speak around the evidence of his arousal.

I wasn't one to blush, but heat crept over my face anyway. He waited patiently as I got out of the bath. At first glance, I thought he was unaffected, but then I noticed the taut line of muscle running up his back. So still. So quiet.

He wasn't breathing.

I pattered across the tile and wrapped myself in a towel. The sound made him release a breath.

"You can turn around now," I said, my voice surprisingly timid. I wasn't used to dealing with fae, much less fae like Lucas.

He glanced at me over his shoulder, as if to confirm I was indeed covered, and then faced me completely, his fangs still out. "I need you to listen to me very carefully," he said, his silver eyes flashing with a glimmer of Light magic. "You have something that I don't."

The heat of his magic reminded me that he was fae, he was everything that was wrong with this world. He was just trying to manipulate me, for what, I hadn't figured out yet, but I was going to do everything I could to make sure he didn't get what he wanted.

"I can think of a few things I have that you're sorely lacking," I said, my words running ahead of my brain. "Manners. Decency. Oh, maybe respect for life?"

If I bothered him, he didn't show it. "You also have access to Malice and an understanding with it that I'll never be able to replicate."

His words came out genuine with a touch of admiration, but I couldn't let myself fall for it. "If you say so."

He smirked, the handsome gesture making butterflies flutter in my stomach. Stupid butterflies. "You're remarkable and I would be a fool to underestimate what you're capable of. Even if you're not a graduate, you'll be able to help the people still trapped along the border."

I chewed my lip before I replied. I couldn't work out why he wanted me to help Dreg-dwellers, but if that was really true, I wasn't going to pass up a chance to save lives. I'd figure out his motives later, for now, if there really were people in danger, I needed to do everything I could to help them.

Plus, if Lucas could teach me how to escape the Academy, that would come in useful later. "Wouldn't that require leaving Academy premises?" I asked, trying not to sound too intrigued by the idea.

He nodded. "Precisely why we have to plan out our little trip for the right moment, effectively and efficiently, and have you back before my father returns or anyone notices."

I raised an eyebrow. "Sounds risky."

He shrugged. "It's not. There will be a break between your remaining classes and my father's return, so I can get you in and out without a problem, as long as we're quick enough."

"And what do you get out of this?"

He smirked. "You truly can't believe me capable of wanting to help humans?"

I shook my head and crossed my arms, careful to make sure my towel stayed plastered to my chest. "Nope. I don't buy it."

He sighed. "Okay, fine. I'll admit, I want to understand you, how you work, how you're able to manipulate Malice when you wear a Crown. It shouldn't be possible, not unless you were a graduate and even then, Malice would be dispersed, not contained and used to your own advantage. You have powers I wish to study."

That sounded more like it.

I nodded. "See? The truth isn't so difficult. You should lead with that next time."

He chuckled as he stepped back into the mists. "I'll work on it."

When he vanished, I shivered, then frowned.

Lucas was up to something bigger than just "studying me," and by all the blasted fae I was going to figure him out.

18

PENNE

*C*ome morning, I couldn't bring myself to wake up Rylie. Seeing her all curled up made her seem far younger than I initially might have guessed. Without that objective scowl to her features, I noticed how her nose turned up at the end, and how her crown glittered atop her tangled curls that shadowed her face. She seemed so helpless and innocent, undeserving of the treatment the fae had given her.

She'd almost died.

Did anyone in her family even care about the kind of danger she was in? No one should have to put up with the fae and their power struggle over Malice like this. It was sickening.

"She's not getting better," hissed Rylie's hand-

198

maiden. The young girl with blonde curls plucked smelling salts from the dresser. "She can't just sleep all day. I'm waking her up."

I snatched the bottle from her grip and stared the girl down. "No you are not," I snarled. "And yes she is getting better. She almost died, for crying out loud. You're not going to wake her up until she has a chance to recuperate, you got that?"

The handmaiden huffed and gathered her skirts. "You're incorrigible! I'm her handmaiden, but if you wish to play the part, then have at it." She jerked her chin over her shoulder and marched out of the room, pausing in the doorway to glare at me. "If she dies on your watch, at least I will be exonerated. She's your responsibility now."

The handmaiden barreled into Olli who tumbled into the room, artifacts loaded in her arms.

"Excuse you!" the woman bit off, then stormed out.

Olli gave me a raised brow and adjusted the bounty in her arms. "Making friends, I see." She glanced at Rylie. "Any change?"

"Some," I said, "but she needs more time."

Olli set the treasures onto the table and closed the door. "Unfortunately, we're all out of that. The

Candidates have been asked to attend an urgent meeting. It's why I came to get you."

I bit my lip, considering if this "meeting" had anything to do with what Lucas had told me. If the King was in the Fae Realm, then I wasn't sure who was going to be watching over the Candidates.

And if I left Rylie alone, who was going to watch over her? Her cheeks had more than regained their color. They were a bit *too* flush and pink.

I rested the back of my hand against Rylie's forehead and jerked back with a hiss. "She's burning up."

Olli hummed, not sounding surprised. "She used a lot of Light, but she'll recover."

"You mean, she needs rest," I finished. It didn't feel like time was on our side.

Olli nodded in agreement, her lips forming a thin line. "If you're worried about her, I can stay and keep watch, but her presence will be expected." Olli glanced back at the door. "No doubt her handmaiden wishes to shove any blame on you. Her fate may be tied to Rylie, but there are loopholes." She gave me a grimace. "If you're not careful, Rylie's handmaiden will pin Rylie's failures on you."

"I don't give two scraps of Malice about her handmaiden." I chewed on my lip. "Where is this meeting, anyway?"

Olli handed me one of the artifacts. "It'll be in the Greenhouse."

I turned the bauble over in my hand. "And what's this for?"

Olli rolled her eyes like I should know that already. "You really need to learn to travel like a proper Princess Candidate." She grabbed my wrist and adjusted my grip so that I held the bauble upright. A golden rune shone when my crown reacted and trickled Light through my body. "Each of these artifacts connects to a place on Academy grounds. And this one…" She popped out a flat artifact from the collection, "will be one for you to use later." She tucked the object into the side of my cleavage, making me squeak.

"Hey!" I exclaimed, but didn't dare let the orb move from where I held it. My crown was too busy fueling it with Light and if I broke its concentration, I had a feeling that I'd be more feverish than Rylie.

"It's a backup artifact to get you to your room. It'll only work for short distances, so don't think you can run off grounds and have a quick jump back— not without an insane amount of Light, anyway."

I frowned, using my free hand to adjust my dress. I would never get used to these outfits. None of my glittering dresses even have pockets, which left the only storage place the side of my cleavage. Whose bright idea was that?

"Right," I said, trying to focus on the matter at hand, "return artifact travel." I gripped the rune harder as I felt a connection forming to someplace just off the main grounds. I sensed life, warmth, and a whole lot of Light.

Olli simply grinned at me when a hum overtook the room. "Have fun," she said with a small wave, "and don't get into too much trouble."

THE WORLD FLASHED with so much Light it left spots streaking across my vision.

When auras of moving forms finally came into view, I realized I wasn't in Rylie's room anymore.

Fingers wrapped over my wrist, making me startle. "Let go of the rune before it blinds you," a female voice chided.

Right.

I dropped the heated orb and the world finally came into focus, revealing a Princess Candidate in a sparkling green dress who politely smiled at me. "I don't believe we've been properly introduced." She extended a hand, fingers down as she displayed her rings. "I am Catherine L'Oranna, youngest of the L'Oranna family."

Right, a true Elite.

Instead of kissing the largest gem on her finger, which I'm sure was an assumption on her part of my station, I gripped her knuckles and gave her a firm shake. "I'm Penne—uh, Penelope, of Rose Academy House."

She took back her hand and gave me a grimace. "How... quaint."

Professor Surin cleared his throat and I realized that I'd teleported into the middle of the Greenhouse and overturned a few plants. "Glad you could join us, Candidate Penelope," he said, glancing at the mess I'd made.

"First time with the runes?" the girl in yellow whispered behind her hand, giving me a sympathetic look.

I shrugged.

Servants quietly cleaned up the overturned dirt and debris while Surin settled himself at a podium. I was tempted to help the servants, but one look at Melinda said she was just waiting for me to screw up. *Go on. Get dirt under your fingernails and show Surin what a fraud you are.*

"We are only missing Candidate Rylie," Professor

Surin observed, sounding bored as he thrummed his fingers over the podium.

"She's still recovering from last night's… dinner," I said, not hiding my disapproval of Rylie's treatment.

The professor narrowed his eyes as his tell-tale golden motes drifted around his face, framing silver hair that swayed over his shoulders. I noted that nothing else moved, not the dresses of the other Candidates or any of the nearby shrubbery, betraying that only Professor Surin enjoyed a cool breeze inside the confines of the stuffy greenhouse. "Are you vouching for her absence?" he asked.

"I am."

He considered me for a moment, then nodded. "Very well. However, I wish to speak with you privately after today's announcements."

The other girls snickered. Ignoring them, Surin began his speech, going on about things I already knew and some things I didn't. The King was in the Fae Realm and would be gone for two weeks, although the reason he supplied was different than the truth Lucas had given me. He'd never said why his father and the other graduates were in the fae realm, and Surin didn't provide much insight on that matter either.

"Extraordinary measures are being taken to ensure your well-being and that of the Kingdom," he supplied, that being the only vague reasoning for the King's absence.

"Is this about the Malice breach?" I asked, surprising everyone as they turned to gawk at me.

Oh, right, I probably wasn't supposed to know about that one.

Surin's curled ears twitched. "Those details are not your concern. As I was saying, all of you will have these two weeks to practice the primary skills that are required of a true Princess Candidate." He indicated the greenhouse display. "A tenacity to elicit life and growth can be practiced here, at the Crown Princess Academy Greenhouse."

Melinda politely coughed. "Or show your proclivities for destruction," she added just low enough for the other candidates to hear as they glanced at me, smothering a new round of giggles.

I rolled my eyes.

Surin continued, although I was sure he had to have heard the snarky brat. "You will also have access to the Music Hall and Weapon's Court. I suggest you visit all three at least once and practice your skills, for when the King returns, we will have a primary exam."

I swallowed hard. Primary exam? We'd only been here a few days, yet it sounded like the fae were in a hurry to process the Queen's Class. Whatever was going on in the Fae Realm had to be bad. I made a mental note to question Lucas about it later.

The Candidate in a glimmering purple dress held up a matching lavender branch, which I realized was growing and blooming right before my eyes. "Like this, Professor Surin?"

The ancient fae gave a slight nod of approval. "Indeed, Candidate Hanna." He clapped his hands. "Now, all of you would be wise to follow Candidate Hanna's example and get to work."

He eyed each of us with a stern brow that told me all I needed to know.

This wasn't practice. This was another test and we were all being watched.

"Candidate Penelope," Professor Surin said, making me flinch. "A word."

THE OTHER GIRLS DISPERSED, some choosing to saunter out in search of the other two locations where Surin said we should practice, while others teleported in a grand show of Light like Melinda.

Only a couple decided to stay, Hanna, the girl in purple, and Catherine, the snooty girl in green. They worked together on various plants and blooms while I followed Surin's shadow, stepping in line with him down the long brush of bounty that thrived in the greenhouse.

I'd never seen such life all in one place. We had the occasional weed and small patch of swampy seaweed that gave us a plant base enough to survive. However, here, I was once again confronted by extravagance and luxury that Elites like Catherine could never truly appreciate.

"You have a wandering eye," Professor Surin observed. "Does Rose Academy House not have a garden? That would seem contrary to its name."

I inwardly cursed how obvious I was being. I might as well shout, *"I'm a Dreg-dweller!"*

Clearing my throat, I thought of a quick coverup. "Oh there are many roses and plant life, however nothing as grand as this. We're a smaller Academy House and we couldn't hope to compete with the fae's grandeur."

Seeming pleased with my response, his fangs retracted a fraction. "I had the chance to speak to the King before his departure to the fae realm."

I winced. "To discuss Rylie?"

He nodded and brushed aside a stray branch that had overgrown the path as we delved deeper into the greenhouse. I glanced back, realizing that we were quite alone now. Not that I suspected Professor Surin had any foul play in mind, or that I couldn't take him on if I really needed to, but it did strike me as odd.

"You have a kindness and charity about you that a Princess Candidate hasn't demonstrated in generations," he said. His flat tone didn't betray how he felt about that. "The King disapproves, therefore I would caution you from showing more compassion than you already have." He paused, noting a smaller bush hidden underneath an overgrowth of ferns. He burrowed into the mass of leaves and extracted the bush trapped in a crate and pulled it closer to the path where the sun could reach it. He wiped his hands on his pristine silver suit, leaving a smudge of dirt down the side. "Not all of us are as impartial as the King. I believe a Crown Princess with a kind heart would be good for the Kingdom, however that is not how the King believes strength against Malice is to be proven. If you wish to survive, I would err on the side of caution, my dear."

I glanced back down the path and then to Professor Surin again, realizing why he'd taken me so far from the others. "If you disagree with the King —" which might as well have been treason "—then why tell me that at all? Why not convince him he's wrong?"

Professor Surin smirked, giving me a glimpse of his eyes crinkling when he smiled. "The King is not one to be persuaded when his mind is made up." He turned his attention to the stain on his suit and sent golden motes to attack the spot, leaving the material glowing until it came away clean, as if the soil had been Malice that needed to be burned. "If you were to graduate, however, I do believe there is some good you could do for this Kingdom."

I had a feeling there was more to the story than Professor Surin was letting on, but he unfurled his palms, revealing two rune stone artifacts. "Now, I encourage you to take today's words to heart and visit the other two practice rooms." He gave me a raised brow, waiting until I accepted the offering, one rune artifact in each hand. "Don't be tempted to visit the Weapon's Court first. While I suspect that will be your favorite, you need to visit all three today to get ahead. I recommend the Music Hall first."

Sighing, I looked at both runes. One was etched with a sword and the other with a music note. I tucked the Weapon's Court rune into my cleavage.

Holding out the remaining rune, I gave Professor Surin a nod. "Thank you for your help."

He gave me a light smile before my crown responded to the artifact, enveloping me in Light and taking me to the rune's destination.

LUCAS

*P*enne appeared in a glorious flash of Light. It didn't surprise me how well she mastered the fae magic without any practice. Well, I imagined that she'd had a lifetime of hardship that had forced that propensity for magic—but on the Malice side. Light wasn't so different. It was just the other side of the coin.

She curled her lip in distaste as the sound of tuning instruments hit her ears. A chuckle threatened to bubble out of me and betray my presence, but I managed to keep myself together.

Hidden.

Secret.

I cloaked myself with Light as I stood against the

wall, invisible to any who weren't fae. Light refracted off of me and made it impossible for the human eye to settle onto me. Even so, I held my breath when Penne's gaze swept over me, pausing just for a moment as if she could see through the illusion.

My heart restarted when she moved on. She gathered her skirts and approached the Princess Candidates who'd made their way to the Music Hall. Gem, the candidate in a golden dress, nursed the broken string on her instrument while a grey-faced Rylie steadied herself on a cushioned chair.

The girl in blue brightened when Penne approached them. "Penelope," she breathed with relief, "your handmaiden told me you covered for me at the greenhouse. Thank you."

Penne frowned. "You should be in bed."

The girl in blue smiled, and while she was weak, she held up a silver flute with pride. "And miss out on getting major score points? I'm from the House of Music, remember? This is my time to shine!"

While Penne rolled her eyes, I noted the way her shoulders relaxed. She'd been worried about the girl. Interesting.

I matched my gaze with Surin, one of the professors who also cloaked himself according to my father's instructions.

Watch the Candidates when they think no one is looking.

Score them accordingly.

My mission that was off the books: Make sure that Penne failed. Surin had unwittingly distracted her so that she hadn't performed any magic in the greenhouse, leaving her with no points. Good.

She *needed* to fail.

Failure meant extra doses of Malice that she would need to accomplish what I had in mind. I couldn't distill Malice myself, nor did I know where my father kept his vials of poison for the candidates. This was the safest and most secure way to get this done.

Even if she hated me for it.

I wasn't sure if I would actually need to intervene when it came to her skill in music. A girl from the Dregs didn't seem the type to be able to carry a tune, but I'd soon find out.

When Rylie started playing her flute, Professor Surin brought out his notepad and jotted down his thoughts. The mesmerizing melody made it hard not to sway and the Candidate from the House of Music did not disappoint her name. When she finished the first refrain, she gave Penne a nod of encouragement.

And then the girl opened her mouth... and sang. I didn't recognize the lyrics, but her skin glowed with a mixture of gold and silver as she instinctively delved into her magic. The music was heartfelt, but something inside of her thrived at the opportunity to express itself in such a pure and beautiful way.

Blessed fae, my heart stuttered and my jaw fell open. Glancing at Surin who was having a similar reaction, I snapped my mouth shut and swiped my hand, making quick work to distort the music so that he wouldn't hear the immense beauty and perfection of her song. It broke a little piece inside of my soul to ruin the moment, but I did it. The sound-waves altered when they hit the barrier I'd put around her and Rylie. To them, they were in an echo chamber of perfect music, but the moment her song hit the invisible wall, it altered just enough to be forced off pitch.

Professor Surin wrinkled his nose and marked down in his notebook with a quick swipe, making me relax.

I waited until the end of Penne and Rylie's song

before slipping into the shadows and heading towards the Weapon's Court where Penne would no doubt make her final appearance—and seal her fate for another hefty dose of Malice when my father returned.

*R*ylie beamed at me when we finished our song. "I couldn't have done better myself," she marveled.

I was just as stunned as she was. The music that came from my soul hardly resembled my own voice and I touched my throat as if I'd find a foreign entity stuck there. Light burned through my veins and told me that something else inside of me had brought out that ancient song.

Yet, the words had come from my soul as if they'd been buried there all along, not created by the foreign crown atop my head.

Shortly after we'd started singing, I'd noticed a shift in the air. I took another compulsory glance around the Music Hall, but Rylie and I were alone. At least, that's what the fae wanted us to think.

"I'm not sure where that came from," I admitted to Rylie. "I guess I just needed your melody to bring it out."

She smiled and settled her silver instrument into her lap. "Would you like to do another?"

As much as I was enjoying my time with Rylie, I couldn't shake the feeling that I was being watched. Surin's warning crept into my mind. I couldn't get too close to the girl, or any of the others—not that anyone else was in danger of my friendship. Only Rylie seemed to be somewhat approachable.

I gave her an apologetic shrug. "I was hoping to go to the Weapon's Court, but why don't you keep practicing here? It seems to be doing wonders for your health."

Rylie stroked the edge of the flute and hummed in agreement. "Music always rejuvenates me." She sighed. "Well, enjoy your weapons, I suppose! I'll be here if you need anything." I turned to leave, but she tugged at my wrist. "Really. Thank you for everything."

I gave her soft fingers a light pat. "You would have done the same for me."

Rylie winced. "I would have been a coward hiding in the corner."

"Nonsense," I chided. "You're too hard on yourself." I gave her fingers a squeeze before stepping away. "Keep practicing, and once you feel up to it, be sure to visit the greenhouse and the Weapon's Court, at least once." I glanced around the room, still unable to shake the feeling that we were being watched. I lowered my voice. "They're calling it practice, but I wouldn't put it past the fae to have spies scoring us before the King returns. Don't let your guard down."

Her eyes widened and she gripped onto the instrument in her lap as if it were a safety line. "Wow, I didn't think of that." She glanced at the door, then back at me, her lips pressed into a thin line. "I'll make sure I only give my best. Thank you, Penelope."

I LEFT the Music Hall feeling both vulnerable and uplifted, but it was time for something familiar.

The sound of metal on metal undid a knot I hadn't even realized was in my shoulders.

It felt like... home.

This was something I could grasp onto. I *knew* combat. I knew how to take a blade and protect myself from a faceless Dreg-dweller out to hurt me.

When I turned the corner and found *who* was sparring in the Weapon's Court, all my relief went right out the window.

Melinda grinned, sword extended, parrying an overly willing fae Prince.

"Lucas?" I gasped, his name coming out of my mouth in a tumble before I could stop myself.

Melinda gave me a raised brow and the fae took advantage of her distraction, moving in for a strike —but he moved too slowly. I knew he was capable of decapitating her with a flick of his wrist if he really wanted to, but he gave Melinda enough time to launch out of the way and swipe away his blade, following the fluid motion with her sword to his throat. "Nice try," she boasted, grinning when Lucas surrendered.

"Are you here to score us, then?" I snapped, not sure exactly why I was so irritated. I knew Lucas was likely here to sabotage any efforts I had at a decent score, but it was the way Melinda seemed so smug to have his attention that made my magic boil in my veins.

"Hardly," he promised, flashing me fang as he winked. That only served to put me in a worse mood. Was he enjoying Melinda's attentions?

Wait, since when did I care?

"The Crown Prince has better things to do with his time," Melinda sneered, trading her sword for a throwing dagger. "As I'm sure you do as well, Candidate Penelope." She danced the blade over her fingers with far more skill than I would have awarded her. "Shouldn't you be in the Music Hall screeching like a cat?"

I knew I shouldn't take the bait, but she made it so easy. "You don't own the Weapon's Court, *Candidate* Melinda. Although it doesn't surprise me you're good with daggers." I gave her a fake smile. "All that practice stabbing people in the back makes for good target practice."

She smirked, clearly amused. Her reply was to turn and toss her dagger, sending it just shy of the center of the bullseye. She propped her hands on her hips and tilted her head, admiring the nearly perfect throw. "Tell you what. If you can match that strike, then I'll let you have Lucas for a sparring partner."

I glanced at the Crown Prince to see if he had anything to say about Melinda claiming she owned such privilege, but he simply shrugged.

Blasted Malice, he was going to be a pain in my side today.

Taking up a dagger from the rack, I closed one eye and hefted the weight in my palm before letting the blade fly.

It should have been a perfect throw, the blade aimed straight at the center of the bullseye that would have put Melinda's attempt to shame. However, an uncharacteristic breeze caught the blade, sending it three rings off center and Melinda barked a laugh.

Blasted Lucas.

"Oh dear. It does look like you need some more practice." She gave me a pout. "Guess I'll be spending more time with the Crown Prince, then."

Magic bubbled up in my chest and it took every ounce of willpower not to hit her with everything I had right there, and Lucas along with her.

I was so tired of being made the fool in this place, being treated like an outsider and having to skulk around like the impostor I was in the Academy.

Revealing myself now over Melinda's petty comments or Lucas's irritating sabotage wasn't going to get me what I wanted. It wouldn't save humanity from Malice or Rylie from the fae.

So I did what any Crown Princess Candidate

would do. I gathered up my skirts, stuck up my nose, and stormed out of the room before I punched both of them in the face.

21

PENNE

*T*he last thing I expected was for Lucas to follow me. I'd gotten halfway down the hall when he grabbed me by the arm and cornered me, slamming both palms on either side of my face.

"Where do you think you're going?" he growled, his fangs elongated and his silver eyes flashing with Light.

Determined not to show any sign of backing down, I raised my chin and didn't flinch away from the danger screaming a warning in his eyes. "What, do you find Melinda boring already? It seemed like you were having a good time sabotaging my throw." I put a finger on my lip. "So, with me, you make me look like an idiot. But with her you let her win. I know you're a better swordsman than that. What am I supposed to make of this?"

He blinked a few times, then a sinister grin overtook his face and he leaned in, making my skin tingle. "Are you... jealous?"

I slammed my palms against his chest and pushed, except that the fae Prince didn't move an inch as his hard core flexed against me. I growled with frustration. "Don't flatter yourself. I'm just tired that every time I turn around you're there making life difficult for me. Why do you want me to fail so badly? If you wanted me dead, there are faster ways to do it." I frowned. "Less annoying ones, too. If you're going to kill me, just get it over with."

He leaned closer until our noses nearly touched and I held my breath. "Do you ever shut up?" he mused.

When I opened my mouth to tell him off, he did the worst thing I could have imagined.

He kissed me.

Lucas's kiss took me by surprise, both in how he crushed his mouth to mine to stifle my complaints, as well as the cool danger of his fangs against my tongue. Stunned, I didn't move until his hand found my ribcage and squeezed.

He pulled away before I could respond and that's when I noticed we had an audience.

Professor Surin cleared his throat. "Prince. I apologize to interrupt, but I was hoping to discuss an important matter."

It hit me why Lucas had kissed me. We were always being watched and he needed an excuse to come talk to me outside of our "secret" meeting place. While I appreciated him taking the effort to talk to me while I had my clothes on, this was a whole new level of personal invasion.

Lucas didn't look away from me as he responded. "I'll be right there, professor. I was just finishing up my conversation with the lovely Candidate Penelope."

Professor Surin snorted, not hiding his disapproval. "Your taste in Candidates is interesting, my prince. This one has the worst score by far."

Lucas shrugged. "What can I say. It's natural to want what we can't have." He ran his thumb down the side of my cheek and I flinched away. "Isn't that right, Penelope?"

Professor Surin snorted and turned to walk away. "I'll see you at your father's study."

It surprised me how the professor seemed to boss Lucas around. When he was out of earshot, I finally pushed the surly prince away. He allowed it this time and grinned at me. "Was all of that really necessary?"

He straightened his suit. "I need you to listen carefully. We will have one opportunity to patch up the breach of Malice at the Dregs and it's when the other professors convene for scoring matchups before my father's return. They'll meet my father in the fae realm for that and I'll be expected to remain here to keep an eye on the Candidates." His tongue flashed across his lips. "I'll just be keeping my eye on you."

I rolled my eyes. "I don't know if I'm buying this. You want to go save a bunch of Dreg-dwellers and risk your father's wrath?" I stabbed a finger at the hallway where the old fae had been just moments before. "And it's clear that you don't have hierarchy around here. The other professors have power over you, or am I wrong?"

He shrugged. "Only until I have a Crown Princess by my side and I take my father's place."

"Which won't be me," I clarified. "You're making sure of that."

"Is that why you think I need you to fail?" he asked, sounding genuinely surprised. "I thought you might have figured me out by now." His grin reappeared. "Or do I need to kiss you again to show you that I have no problem with you being the sole graduate of the Queen's Class?"

I growled, hating how my stomach flipped at the memory of his mouth on mine. "That won't be necessary."

"Good," he said, straightening one of his cuffs. "Then I recommend you keep yourself occupied in your room for the remainder of the practice period as much as possible. You've already been scored by Professor Surin and it's best if you keep out of sight so you don't ruin all my work.

I blinked at him. "The Music Hall," I began. "I felt someone watching..." Had he sabotaged me, even then? Had Professor Surin been listening? If so, my score should have been fine, more than fine. However, the satisfied look on Lucas's face said otherwise.

"I'll see you in two weeks," he said with finality, and then turned and left me alone, reeling from a mixture of emotions that confused me more than if he'd said he wished me dead.

The fae Prince was interested in me, that much

was clear, and he had an agenda when it came to his father and the Queen's class. One that involved me... one that I was determined to figure out.

22
PENNE

*T*wo weeks later

Staying in my room for two weeks straight would have made me go straight-up insane had I not had a project to work on. Olli and I needed enough time to find an artifact not permitted for general Candidate use. While I was breaking rules, I tried to get a letter to Jilly, but of course that was intercepted. Professor Surin had given me a good scowl and sent me off with negative marks to add to my already abysmal score.

"Did you find it?" I asked Olli with a giddy sense of excitement. I'd been working with Olli for two weeks to find not just any artifact, but a particular one that would give me an explosive blast of Light. It was all part of my grand plan to get Zizi back.

The artifact proved difficult to find. We'd narrowed it down to a locked study, so good thing I was a good lock-pick. I'd left the door unlocked, leaving Olli to do the recon. She promised it was less risky if she got caught instead of me.

This was my one chance at getting something back that was missing from this equation.

Zizi.

My dark manifestation of Malice could be annoying at times, but I didn't realize how much I missed her until she was gone. I needed her advice when it came to Lucas. She would know what to do. I had one week before I was about to have to trust him—something I was not very keen on doing.

Olli smiled and handed me the translucent rune-stone. It had taken us nearly the entire two weeks before the Fae King's return to find the artifact. "You owe me, big time."

Grinning, I took it and turned it over. I opened my mouth to ask her a question, then thought better of it and snatched up our shared notepad. I jotted down my question as fast as I could.

Are you sure this'll work? It'll disable any spy magic in this room?

She read the note when I presented it to her, then nodded while pointing to my crown.

The answer was clear. Yes, it would work, but I'd have to use my Light magic to make it happen.

I didn't really care if Professor Surin realized that I had disabled any attempts of spying in my room. That would require him admitting to it in the first place, which I doubted he would do. Besides, he still would never guess what I was really up to. I mean, conjuring a pixie manifested of raw Malice wasn't exactly something Candidate Princesses did every day, but if I could bring Zizi back, perhaps I could figure out what Lucas was really up to.

Plus, I really needed a friend who knew the old me.

"Okay, close your eyes," I warned Olli, then focused all of my energy onto the stone.

My crown responded immediately, flooding me with Light and illuminating the room with a blaze of heat. I'd gotten better at tapping into the raw fae magic. It was the exact opposite of Malice, and once I'd figured that out, it helped to know how to master it.

Light wanted to burn, destroy, cleanse and reform anything it touched into its own idea of perfection. Using its magic was easy—I just needed to give it an object to purify. In this case, the stone in my hand.

The rune flared to life and soon revealed three orbs stuck to the ceiling that had been previously invisible. They cracked and fell to the floor in a shattered mess of magic and glass.

Olli jumped at the sound, but she didn't open her eyes. "What was that?" she hissed.

I chuckled and dropped the stone that had started to sizzle, job done. "*That* was Professor Surin losing his little spy orbs." I doubted the orbs had visuals, given that we'd been passing notes back and forth for days without incident, but it was nice to be able to speak freely.

Olli peeked one eye open, glanced around the room, and then relaxed. "Well done, Penne." She smiled, having grown more friendly with me after our time together. I still didn't completely trust her, but she was making strides in that venture. Helping me disable the spy orbs in my room certainly didn't hurt.

However, as much as I was growing fond of her, I wasn't ready to reveal my true nature, not yet.

Giving her an apologetic smile, I patted her on the shoulder. "Now that I know no one's listening, there's something I need to do—alone."

Hurt crossed her expression, but she didn't fight

me on it, and instead gave me a brief nod. "I'll scope out how the other Candidates are doing before the King's return."

I relaxed. "Thanks, Olli. I'm glad you understand."

I waited until the door clicked closed, Olli leaving me to my own devices, before releasing the breath I'd been holding.

Right. Time to do this before Lucas catches on it's safe to talk to me in my room.

He hadn't bothered me over the past two weeks, making me nervous as to what he was really up to. Even if I had obeyed him and stayed in my room as much as possible, I still expected him to invade my bath chamber for more of our secret conversations. After the romantic development of our relationship, a part of me was anxious about that and what he might do. I wasn't sure if I was relieved or disappointed that he hadn't appeared.

Well, all the more reason to summon Zizi. If I was actually disappointed that the Crown Prince wasn't creeping on me while I took a bath, then I definitely had been wearing this stupid crown for far too long.

I'd never banished Zizi before, so summoning her was a bit of a quandary, but I tried anyway. I curled my feet under me as I sat on the floor and thought about attempting to remove my crown. It allowed me freedom now and again, but it burned against my head after having used it on the rune-stone. It was hungry for my attention and wouldn't be unseated just yet.

"Fine," I grumbled, rubbing at the heated metal of the tiny crown. "You just don't get in my way, yeah?"

I took the lack of response for agreement as I closed my eyes and concentrated. I reached into myself like I had done so many times before, finding the cold Malice permanently embedded in my heart and coaxing it out of its hiding place. It didn't want to leave the cocoon I'd made for it, not with my crown keeping an eye on it at all times, however the two forces were coming to an understanding inside my body. There was a place for both and I refused to allow one side to wipe out the other. Because of the crown, I had more Light in my body than I knew what to do with, but Malice had always been a part of my life and it would be the more powerful force if I could figure out how to properly wield it while I wore my crown.

This was the perfect kind of practice I needed to master my unique magic. If Lucas—or anyone else—

tried to come after me, I needed to be able to defend myself. With the way Lucas kept sabotaging my scores, I would also be forced to drink more and more Malice, enough that could kill me if I wasn't ready for it.

No way was that going to happen. I had survived all my life embracing Malice and coaxing it to my own will instead of succumbing to its darker nature and I wasn't going to stop now.

I concentrated, searching for that dark tingling sensation when Malice collected. My extremities went cold and I flexed my fingers.

A flicker of recognition swept through my body and I snapped my eyes open. "Zizi?" I hissed.

A shadow manifested in front of me and I held my breath, waiting to see if my attempts had worked. The dark ball writhed and a small flutter of wings flitted around the edges, making me lean forward with anticipation. I was so excited to see Zizi again that I didn't notice the glow inside of the shadow until an entirely new creature popped out.

I jumped back when the Light pixie tumbled onto the carpet, stopping just shy of my knees as she grabbed her head and looked up at me with a pained expression. "Ow, that hurt!" she complained, then brushed powdered Light from her impossibly tiny dress. She tested her fluorescent wings a few times before hovering a few inches off the ground. She flitted up to my face and gave me a small curtsey and a big smile. "Hello, I'm Laurel, nice to meet you!"

A LIGHT PIXIE. Of all the manifestations of power I could have summoned, why did it have to be a Light pixie?

I didn't think that she was dangerous, but if she didn't shut up I might just kill myself.

"I've been trapped in that crown for centuries! Do you know what centuries feels like? Of course not, you're human so you don't live very long. Does that terrify you? No wonder humans are so grouchy all the time. Knowing you're going to die in a blink of an eye would put anyone in a bad mood. I guess I can't blame you for it. Maybe if—"

I rubbed a hand over my face.

"What?" she exclaimed. "You're not going to die now, are you?"

"I wouldn't rule that out," I grumbled, then sighed. "Where's Zizi?"

The Light pixie tilted her head, the motion sounding a tiny jingle. "What's a Zizi?"

My hackles rose, because I doubted a Light pixie was stupid. "She's a Malice pixie, kind of like you."

Her eyes went wide. "Malice? Malice! I have nothing to do with Malice!"

I frowned. "There's both Malice and Light in my body. If you were in my crown, then you've been trying to kill off the Malice in me for over two weeks. Is it because you wanted to get to Zizi? Is that why you've been so difficult?"

The Light pixie flitted about the room and tugged at the closed drapes. I snatched the cloth from her to keep her from opening them. She propped her hands on her tiny hips. "I don't know any Zizi!" she insisted.

"I don't believe you," I growled and snatched for the creature. "You better not have hurt her!"

Laurel zoomed out of range. "I've never met a Crown Princess who was so rude! I'd never hurt anybody!"

"*Candidate* Crown Princess," I corrected and glared. "And I highly doubt that. Have you even *met* the power which created you? Light is vicious and merciless. Which is exactly why I need to talk to Zizi. I have one day left before the Fae King returns and Malice knows what kind of score I have for the Queen's Class. Lucas wants to take me off campus to banish Malice from a border breach to the Kingdom and I have a feeling the unsanctioned trip will have repercussions I'm not prepared to deal with. I need advice—advice someone like you isn't going to be able to help me with."

Her eyes went wide, revealing tiny golden sparkles around her irises. "Advice concerning the Crown Prince? Well why didn't you say so!" Laurel tapped her mouth that had puckered into a small pout. "Well, I've been watching from the crown and I can assure you that the Crown Prince doesn't mean you harm. He's one of the good ones, you know." She folded her hands to the side of her head and gave a dreamy sigh. "He made sure I found you, after all. He didn't leave me in that dusty treasure room to rot away, even when all the other crowns had already been picked!"

A knock on the door had us both jumping. I glared at the pixie and pointed at the crown. "Well, back you go! Unless you want us both to get busted."

She shivered as if the idea of returning to the crown repulsed her, but when another knock sounded, she curled her shoulders before relenting and flitted up to my head. In a flash of light she had been reabsorbed by the crown.

Testing my fingers over the warmed metal, I nodded in satisfaction and then opened the door, only to find an annoyed Crown Prince glaring down his nose at me. "I thought I told you to keep a low profile?"

He shoved his way inside and I squeaked in surprise as he slammed the door closed. "Well, come on in, then! Not like this is my room or anything."

He frowned and took note of the smashed spy orbs still littering the ground. "How did you even banish them? Now Surin is going to be watching us and we're supposed to leave soon." He sighed. "I'm going to have to think of a way to distract him. Damn it, Princess, you create more trouble than you're worth sometimes."

I crossed my arms, which was always a bit of a challenge to do with my boned magical dress that insisted I keep my shoulders rolled back and my head held high. It tugged at my unladylike posture more than usual, making me flinch.

Laurel was already causing trouble.

I unfurled my arms to appease the tingling sensation running up my spine. She didn't talk to me in my head like Zizi sometimes did, but I felt her insistence that I could trust Lucas, even if every one of my own instincts told me not to. Laurel hadn't done anything to win my trust, so I wasn't about to listen to her. "I'm tired of being spied on," I snapped. "There's no way I was going to let anyone listen in on me in my own bedroom. Do the other girls know about this invasion of privacy?"

Lucas rubbed his temples. "I'm sure they don't. None of them are half as intuitive as you are."

Flushing at the unexpected compliment, I frowned. "I'm surprised you even dignified me with a knock before barging into my room. You might try to play the gentleman, but you fae are all the same."

That seemed to strike a nerve. Lucas's fangs extended and he rushed me, pinning me against the wall with a growl. "Never compare me to the fae. I'm not like the rest of them."

Usually I was quick on my feet, but perhaps two weeks sitting on my toes had made me weak. The prince had thrown me off guard and my head throbbed where it had hit the wall. I winced and ran my fingers over the wound. I hissed when they came back red with blood.

"You prove my point, *my Prince.*"

Lucas stared down at the blood, his canines retreating. "I didn't mean—"

I shoved him away. He stumbled back, daring to give me a hurt expression. "You're just like the rest of them. I don't care what you think of yourself. You treat everyone around you like a toy, and when you're done with it, you're just going to throw it away."

He stared me down, but he didn't tell me I was wrong. "Be ready to go in an hour," he said, then stormed out of the room before I could protest.

Laurel appeared in a puff of golden glitter and gave me a smirk. "He's soooo into you."

I rolled my eyes. "Whatever."

Maybe he was, and I was going to use that to my advantage. I'd had two whole weeks to think of what my next move was going to be, and Lucas had proven to me what I needed to do.

I needed to kill the Crown Prince.

It was so simple. I couldn't believe I hadn't seen it sooner.

No Crown Prince.

No unholy union.

No more Queen's Class graduates or Royal Line to propagate.

Even if I didn't understand fae politics, it was clear that they placed huge value on a human and fae marriage to bring forth a child. I didn't know what kind of deal the fae got out of it, but I had no doubt it gave humanity the short end of the stick.

When Lucas took me off of Academy grounds, I had the perfect opportunity. Not only would I cast the Academy into chaos, but I'd be able to escape and plan my next move.

I was going to end this once and for all.

*B*lasted female.

She was going to be the death of me.

I wanted to tell Penne everything, but that would just put her in more danger, and now that Professor Surin had his eye on me, things were just going to be worse. If I did get caught, it would be best if she didn't know what I'd been up to.

For the past two weeks I'd been ransacking my father's hidden treasure caches to get enough Light crystals to keep her and all the other Candidates alive when my father returned. Something had been off about him before he'd left. He was up to something and whatever it was, it wasn't going to be good.

We didn't have much time left. I had to expose Penne to the Malice she needed to stand up to the fae. She was about to get a massive dose of Malice at the primary exam results. She wouldn't be ready, not without a little boost first.

"Thanks to your little stunt, we have to travel the forest at night," I growled, shifting on my horse as we slipped into the darkness. "Do you know what kind of creatures come out at night?"

"Oh I don't know," she spat back, squirming in my grip, "ones that eat arrogant fae princes?"

I squeezed around her middle with warning. She wanted to test my boundaries. Tonight, I wasn't going to play her game. Too much was at stake. "Professor Surin has asked to speak to me in the morning, no doubt about your antics. So we need to do this before sunrise."

"Do what, exactly?" she asked, still squirming as she tried to get away from me. Stubborn female. "Are you trying to suffocate me? Because it's working."

"I'm not going to let you escape me and get yourself killed." I had already spotted two predators watching us from the foliage. The Light in my body swirled with warning, pulsating an invisible ward that kept them at bay. It was working, but not if enough creatures banned together to overwhelm us. We had to be quick about it.

"The only danger I'm in is from the Academy." She twisted to glare at me. "And you."

The Academy? Yes. That was one of the most dangerous places in the human realm. But me? I would never hurt her. "I'm trying to protect you."

"Sure you are," she said, turning her gaze forward into the darkness. "If by protect me, you mean squeeze me to death and put off enough heat to make me melt on this horse, then yes, you're doing a fabulous job of protecting me."

Right, she would be able to feel my magic, but there wasn't much I could do about that. "I'm keeping the predators away. We're being watched."

She huffed. "You just don't want me running off. I'm not going to be scared into compliance by some bedtime story of monsters creeping in the forest." She threw up her hands. "What, are some conjured butterflies going to flutter me to death?"

Another set of eyes appeared in the darkness, two yellow orbs that winked in and out of existence. My stallion cantered to the left and whinnied.

Crap.

Animals had a keen sense when it came to predators.

"If you can feel what I'm doing, can you add your Light to mine? I would like to get out of this forest alive."

She stilled in my grip, tormenting me as her body relaxed against mine, moving with the beast's steps. She flinched when those yellow eyes appeared again, this time more brazen. The predators were toying with us, which meant they were going to strike any second now. "What is that?" she asked, her voice rising a pitch. "Seriously. What the Malice is that?"

I smirked. "Oh, so now you believe me."

"Okay, maybe I believe you. What do you need me to do?"

Before I could instruct her, the horse jerked to the side, making me grab onto Penne to keep her from falling.

An alpha beast emerged from the forest and skidded onto the path.

A panther.

The forest was a safe haven for what had been majestic animals in the human realm, but generations and lifetimes exposed to the forest's relentless magic had changed them, made them bigger, stronger, and more intelligent.

Panthers might have been lone beasts, but in the

forest they worked together, communicating with sharp clicks as they coordinated their attack. They normally preyed on other forest animals, but tonight, we were on the menu.

"New tactic," I said, sending a surge of Light building in my body, "we make a run for it."

"What?" she asked, then shrieked as I slammed my heels into the sides of my horse.

"Yah!"

I fueled my beast with magic, giving him a boost of speed as we surged around the panther. The animal lunged at us, claws extended, and yellow eyes full of wild rage.

The hunt was on.

I clasped my thighs to the horse and clung Penne to me, clutching her close to my chest as she surprised me by giving over her Light magic to aid our plight. She hadn't taken Professor Surin's class of Light Development yet, but her relationship with magic gave her an edge. She had the instincts needed to become a master and I lamented that things couldn't be different. If the fae weren't so horrible, if there weren't so many secrets and hidden agendas, perhaps she could have been my queen.

I was so fixated on Penne that I failed to notice

one of the beasts waiting in ambush. Sharp claws and slick black fur blurred, slicing across my vision as pain exploded in my side. The world turned upside down as the massive beast launched me off of my horse.

All I could hear were Penne's screams.

PENNE

I should have let the prince die. This was the perfect opportunity. I didn't even have to do anything; a mutated panther enhanced by magic was going to end him for me.

But… I couldn't let that happen.

Something inside of me knew this was wrong. No matter my calculations or plans, I always listened to that little niggling voice in my head. Maybe it was Zizi, or even Laurel, but I knew I couldn't just sit back and watch.

I couldn't let him die.

For the first time since I'd put on my crown, Malice gathered in my chest and launched from my fingertips, sending a blast at the panther and stunning the beast. Those yellow eyes locked on me as he roared. I balked at the display of its impressive teeth still red from its last kill, but this wasn't the first time I'd faced death. A lifetime of being bullied by Malice Casters, surviving the gang of the Northern Sector, and clawing my way up as one of Gavin's best made me a force to be reckoned with.

Malice gathered in me again, this time threaded with the heat of my Light magic, and hit the creature again.

It screeched as it skidded back from the blow. A few of its hunting mates lingered in the shadows, waiting to see what their Alpha would do.

It shook its head, snarled, then decided we weren't worth it and disappeared into the forest in a shimmering of magic and sleek fur.

Taking stock of my injuries, I gasped for breath. Being flung from the horse had knocked the wind out of me, and my left ankle raged with pain, but otherwise I was unharmed.

Lucas, though, was not so lucky.

A long gash ran the full length of his side and he groaned as he clutched at it, pulling himself up against a tree. I scrambled over to him. His horse had run off back towards the Academy, so we were stranded here.

Great.

"Can you close the wounds?" I asked him. I'd used Malice to heal injuries before, kind of like a magical cauterizing tactic, but I didn't want to use that on the prince. As a fae, I didn't know what effect Malice magic would have on him, and I didn't want to test my newfound skills with the Light.

He bit off a curse. "No," he ground out the word. "The beast. It—" he hissed with pain, doubling over again.

Then I noticed it. The creature had poisoned him with Malice, leaving tiny shards of darkness lodged into his skin. Perhaps Lucas could have healed a normal wound, but not this.

I was going to have to burn it out.

Without hesitation, I tugged at his vest and peeled what was left of it off. "I'm going to help you, but it's going to hurt," I warned him.

His blue eyes flashed up to meet mine. It surprised me that I saw trust. He relaxed, arching his neck and exposing the full length of his wound. "Do it."

I assessed the damage as I ran my fingertips over his broken skin. The slash hadn't gone too deep, intending to stun him rather than kill him outright.

The panther had wanted to play with his food. "Don't move."

The prince nodded, then closed his eyes.

I reached out for the Malice in his body, calling it to me. It responded instantly, grateful for a purpose and a home. This was my relationship with Malice. I would be its conduit and I would use it to help others. The tiny shards seeped from his wound. It impressed me that the Prince didn't move, didn't cry out. I knew it must have been agonizing as I worked the slow magic to extract the Malice from his body.

Once it was done, I glanced up at his face. The only evidence of his exertion was the layer of sweat over his high cheekbones. "Can you heal the wound now? I've removed the poison."

He took in a shaky breath and furrowed his brows in concentration. A fine glistening of Light swept over his body and the wounds began to close.

Impressive.

If I could master my Light, could I help others like this? Malice healing was always messy and painful, but the way Lucas relaxed when his skin stitched closed made me hopeful.

"Penne?" he asked, surprising me by using my preferred name.

"Yes?"

"Come here." He winced as he leaned against the twisted tree. There was too much blood for me to tell if he'd completely healed. Perhaps he needed another boost of my Light.

I leaned in. "What is it?"

He opened his eyes, making my breath catch before he closed the short distance between us as his lips found mine.

Blasted fae.

His hand went to my hip, bringing me closer to him. When I didn't pull away, he deepened the kiss and threaded his fingers through my hair.

The moment might have been romantic until he nicked my crown and a zap of unpleasant heat surged through me. He flinched away, then grinned.

"Your crown is bossy."

"Tell me about it," I growled.

What gives? I thought at my crown, knowing that Laurel was listening to me. *I thought you adored the prince. You should be happy he kissed me.*

He can kiss you all he wants... Came a tiny voice in my head, *when I don't have to see it!*

Wow, such a prude.

"It's talking to you, isn't it?" Lucas asked with a sexy grin. "What's it saying? Am I being bad?" His extended canines flashed as his grin grew. "Very, very bad?"

"Shut up," I grumbled, but couldn't fight a tiny smile that lit my face.

I couldn't remember the last time I'd really smiled. Maybe there was something to the prince I hadn't considered.

Then I realized all my plans had just been obliterated.

All because of a kiss.

"What's wrong?" he asked, his tone turning concerned.

I looked down the dark path. We'd been on the road long enough that we couldn't turn back to the Academy. We were going to have to make our way to the Kingdom and find another way back. There was no way I was going to walk in the forest longer than I had to and wait to be attacked again. Not to mention, I needed to come up with another way to bring the Academy down if I wasn't going to kill the prince. "We need to get out of here. This place creeps me out."

He got to his feet, making me blush as he flashed with Light to remove the blood, which revealed a killer set of abs and an attractive "V" that disappeared into his waistband. Malice, why did he have to be so perfect? It'd be so much easier if I could just kill him.

"You're right," he said, pretending to be oblivious that I was totally checking him out. He sauntered down the path. "We still have a mission to complete. We better get on with it."

I wasn't sure what I expected the prince to show me, but the last thing I really expected was the truth.

Malice indeed had encroached on Kingdom territory and curled over itself in murky wisps. I was used to seeing breaches like this in the Dregs, but I always figured the Kingdom had some kind of magical privilege to avoid the toxic invasion.

I wasn't afraid of Malice. Even though I had Light magic in me now, nothing had changed when it came to my relationship with the ever-present shadow that lived in my chest. Lucas made a strained sound when I marched up to the inky blackness, but relaxed as I ran my fingers over it.

"It's dense," I observed. "Too big for me to move."

Lucas kept his distance. "Are you sure you should be touching it?"

I cast a glance over my shoulder. The fae watched me with unerring watchfulness. I wasn't sure what he thought he could do should I succumb to Malice, but I appreciated his concern. "I'm not ingesting it," I reminded him. "Malice on the outside won't harm me. It's when it's shoved down my throat without warning that I have difficulties."

He smirked. "My apologies for that. Can't be helped."

Right.

Rolling my eyes, I turned back to the damage. "I'm not sure what you expect me to do. The encroachment path is huge and clearly has been here for at least a month. That's long enough for the Malice to soak into the ground and stake its claim."

Without a proper host, Malice would make its home in the very soil it contaminated. The first thing I learned as a Malice Caster was the longer Malice had condensed on an area, the more difficult it would be to manipulate.

Movement caught my eye, catching a glimpse of a woman dashing through moving safe pockets. I watched her, mesmerized that someone would be dumb enough to brave lethal Malice like this. If she were a Malice Caster, she would have walked straight through it, but it was clear she wasn't.

Then I saw where she was going.

"Someone's injured over there," I said, pointing at a dark form crouching on a hill. The shadows shifted, allowing me to see a man who frantically waved the woman to leave him alone. The way she ignored him and tilted a skin of water over his mouth said that she would walk through death for him—in fact she had. They must be husband and wife.

Lucas dared a few steps closer and then cursed. "I thought they'd all gotten out."

I whirled on him. "What? Who had gotten out?"

He sighed and rubbed the back of his neck. "The last time I was here, there were some people trapped on the hill. I made a path for them to escape, but I didn't realize one of them had been injured."

I balked. This poor woman would have been going back and forth for over two weeks trying to keep her husband alive. "We have to do something."

Lucas nodded. "I agree. That's why we're here."

"You said you didn't know there was anyone trapped."

"Of course, but I meant I brought you here to

disperse the Malice. It's stabilized a pocket, yes? Won't it just endanger more of your people?"

This was a prime location, a hub between the West and Southern Sectors normally filled with traffic. Lucas was right, if this Malice was allowed to spread any further, Dreg-dwellers would be forced to brave the miasma just to keep doing business.

I narrowed my eyes. "Disperse the Malice? I thought only Academy graduates could do that." This was all just a giant waste of time. If Lucas had brought me here to kill me, there were faster ways to do it.

He held out his hand. His jaw flexed as his canines extended, this time I guessed out of irritation. "When are you going to start trusting me?"

"You're a fae," I reminded him. That was all the explanation needed. I could never trust him, because I could never trust the very race that put all of humanity on a path to extinction. They liked to paint a pretty picture that Malice had come into existence of its own accord and they were our valiant protectors, but come on, I wasn't stupid.

He didn't budge. "I think you know I'm not like other fae."

I considered him, taking a moment to think about that. He looked like a fae in every perfectly obnoxious way possible. Pointed Ears. Sharp fangs. And without his shirt, an athletic body that made my eyes want to wander. He had a stature that made him seem regal, not to mention the glowing circlet on his brow that marked him as a prince. He was so completely off the map of normal that it hurt.

Yet, I wanted to trust him.

Instead of judging him by his appearance, I tried to dig deeper. He had an agenda that he hadn't fully shared with me, that much was for sure, but he also took risks. He didn't let Professor Surin know I had disabled the spy orbs. He was making sure I was given the highest doses of Malice possible at the Academy, which in all reality was only going to make me stronger. If he was able to read me well enough, if he really knew I was a powerful Malice Caster, then he knew I was strong enough to handle it.

Which meant he wasn't trying to kill me.

So what the heck was he up to?

"How can I trust you if you aren't honest with me?" I pressed, slapping his hand away and stepping closer to him. Malice hissed around my feet as I commanded it to slip around us.

Lucas should have been afraid. Instead, he straightened, trusting me to not allow the Malice to touch his skin. Glittering golden magic sparkled across his skin, reacting to the darkness. It made him look so ethereal and beautiful that I could cry.

"I've been nothing but honest with you," he protested. "What do you want to know? I have nothing to hide."

I chewed my lip. "Why do you want me to fail my classes?"

"So that you'll be given full doses of Malice. I thought that much was apparent."

I narrowed my eyes. "Yes, but why?"

A screech interrupted us, the woman crying out as she dragged her injured husband away from an encroaching sliver of Malice.

"Could we do this another time?" Lucas asked as he presented his hand again. "You don't need to be a graduate to disperse Malice. All you need is to be able to use artifacts, which I know you're more than capable of doing." He impatiently flexed his fingers. "What the professors will never teach you is that the fae can be used as conduits for magic, essentially behave as living artifacts for your power. You can use my Light to disperse the Malice, all you have to do is trust me."

My jaw dropped. Was he serious?

I wanted to ask more questions, or at least call

him out for being vague and irritating, but another scream from the woman demanded I didn't wait any longer. I grabbed the prince's hand and opened my walls, letting him in.

Light flooded into me without warning and my head snapped back from the impact. Heat billowed out around me, hissing and burning the nearby Malice that kissed my skin. My crown welcomed the invasion of power, but the Malice in my chest tightened like a wounded animal, curling in on itself and wailing in panic.

Lucas tightened his grip on me as he directed his magic. Better than an artifact, he guided the raw power that crashed into me, helping me to work the Light to my will.

Burn.

Destroy.

Protect.

The Light had a mind of its own, but dispersing Malice was on the list of its top ten favorite things to do.

Saving humans was a close second.

Within moments the Malice uprooted from what I would have thought to be a permanent hold as it retreated and dissolved. Everywhere I looked Light billowed out of me in growing waves. The people I was trying to save were there, small figures as they retreated to safety.

Good. Two Dreg-dwellers who would survive in a world where Malice took so many lives.

Elated with that achievement, I let my guard down.

Big mistake.

"Slow it down," Lucas grit out, but it was too late. Light hummed with an increasing frantic pitch and my fingertips began to burn. I tried to pull it back, but the magic had a mind of its own.

"Let go!" I shouted as Lucas's grip on me turned into a branding hot iron. "You're hurting me!"

"Can't!" he shot back, sounding just as pained as I was.

Holy fae on a ferry. This wasn't good.

Burning sensations swept through my body and brought me to my knees. I cried out, only to have the sound swept up in a firestorm of power. Nearly all of the Malice had been dispersed in this quadrant, but the price for that was going to be a Penne-shaped burn mark on the street.

Penne! a tiny voice shouted, and my heart leapt to hear Zizi again.

"Zizi! Are you all right?"

Am I all right? Girl, you're about to implode! Get your

butt in a Malice bubble before the Light finishes off the last of the Malice in this area. It's going to come for me next!

I gasped. Of course. The mission had been to disperse Malice, but the problem with that was I had a pocket of Malice lodged permanently in my body. I knew it could never be removed, not without killing me, and if the burning waves of scalding power through my body were any indication, I didn't have much time left.

Lucas couldn't let go of my hand, but he yanked me into his chest as if to protect me from his own magic. "I'm so sorry," he growled in my ear. "I shouldn't have risked this. I thought—"

I didn't care what excuse Lucas had for me. I was going to die if I didn't do something right now.

A familiar cold sensation pulsed deep beneath the layers of hot pain. The Malice was calling me—no, someone was calling me.

A hand extended in my mind with wisps of soothing cool darkness writhing around it. I didn't need any further encouragement.

I closed my eyes and accepted the invitation.

LUCAS

*I*t all happened so fast. I knew that Penne was strong, but I had no idea that she would be able to rip my ancestral magic out of me so quickly, and so thoroughly.

She was born for this.

Hopefully she'd survive it.

I knew that this kind of magic exchange would be detected by the fae, so I needed a valid excuse for allowing Penne to access my power. Dispersing Malice encroaching on my territory was as good an excuse as any, which was why I had brought her here in the first place. Better to act pompous and arrogant than ask for permission to take her off Academy grounds.

The fact that it helped her people was a bonus.

There was a reason to my method, one I wasn't ready to share with Penne yet. I needed her to be strong enough for the next dose of Malice, for what would come at the primary exam. By having access to the royal line of Light in my body, she should have gotten a boost.

Instead, she'd gone supernova.

"What have I done?" I whispered, running my fingers over the scars on the street where Penne had been just a moment before. My nostrils flared, searching for the intoxicating scent of her, but all I could detect was the raw metallic remnants of burnt Malice.

No, she couldn't be dead. I refused to believe that. She was far too strong—and stubborn.

The black streaks across the ground suggested otherwise.

A strange sensation spread across my chest, sending shivers down my spine. I didn't recognize the emotions at first, then realized it was fear, dread, and panic. I always kept it together, but the thought of losing Penne like this made bile rise in my throat. A hard swallow helped me to keep the bitterness down.

Right, get it together.

Penne couldn't have just evaporated. That display

of clashing magic would have left more than just black streaks behind. I took three deep breaths and then concentrated. My magic crept to the surface of my skin, hesitant and wary. I couldn't shake the feeling that I'd hurt Penne, but I couldn't think about that right now. I had to believe she was okay.

When Light warmed my body and illuminated the foggy streets, I spotted it. The telltale warped air of a vortex portal.

I let out a sigh of relief. She wasn't dead. She'd teleported.

Okay, so where exactly did she go?

I stepped closer to the scar that wavered across my vision. Teleportation always left behind a remnant, but a true scar like this meant she hadn't just traveled a long distance, she'd traveled across realms. A flush of irritation swept over me. What was she thinking? There were rules about realm travel, especially dire if she'd encroached on fae territory. A closer inspection said she hadn't gone to the Fae realm. There were no sparks of gold anywhere to be seen. Where else then, could she have gone? There were seven realms, some less pleasant than others.

Icy dread curled in my stomach as I ran a finger over the scar. I braved a moment of pain as I closed my eyes and spread the scar like a curtain to the other realm. I wouldn't be able to follow her this way, not without using the same amount of energy that she'd just expended, but I would be able to glimpse a peek.

Darkness.

Death.

Chaos.

My eyes snapped open.

Of all the realms... she'd gone to the worst one of all.

The birthplace of Malice itself.

"*W*elcome home, sweetheart."

I knew that voice.

"Who the Malice are you?" I snapped, but I knew who it was. I'd heard that voice invading my thoughts all my life.

Steel.

The fae before me dripped with Malice, as well as a sense of smugness that was all too familiar. Even if I'd never seen his face—which was drop-dead gorgeous—I would recognize that snide grin anywhere.

He brought a hand to his chest. "Oh, darling, I'm wounded."

I propped my hands on my hips. "Doubt it." Sighing, I glanced at our surroundings which were finally starting to come into focus. It felt like I'd had my face stuck in broad sunlight all my life and that light had suddenly been snuffed out, leaving only delicate silver moonlight to illuminate my surroundings.

I was no longer at the edge of the Kingdom facing a breach. Now, I stood in a wide-open space under the stars. We were indoors, I could tell because there was no breeze and towering walls framed us on all sides, but the ceiling caught my attention. It was made of glass and allowed a spectacular view to the stars, yet the grandeur was broken by wisps of blackness that licked at the barrier trying to get in.

"Is that Malice?" I asked. It surprised me how steady my voice came out. Perhaps I was in shock. I'd just traveled somewhere, and I had a sense that it was much farther from the Dregs or even the Kingdom than I could have imagined. Was I in the Outlands beyond the Dregs? There wasn't supposed to be anyone left alive. Surely a place like this would have been discovered. A sanctuary among Malice.

"Yes," Steel said, effortlessly looping an arm around my waist and drawing me closer to him as he gazed up at the ceiling. "Isn't it beautiful? It really dances this time of day."

"Day?" I asked, balking. Surely it was the middle of the night.

He chuckled. "Oh yes. You'll know when it's nighttime in the Malice Realm because you won't be able to see a thing." He kissed me on the nose. "But then I could have just been a disembodied voice to you again. Might have felt a bit more familiar, yeah?"

I blinked a few times, then remembered to breathe.

Malice Realm.

What... the fae.

28

LUCAS

First, damage control. Penne was in the Malice Realm. Professor Surin, who was definitely reporting back to my father my every move, would expect an explanation. I'd already counted on him sensing a flux of magic, however I hadn't expected for Penne to up and vanish.

Various plans unfurled in my mind, but each one counted on the fact that Penne would return to me. She had twelve hours before her absence would be noticed. If she didn't show up for the Primary Exam results, then any lie I constructed would fall apart.

No one escaped the Academy. It would be obvious that I'd helped her. The only way out was through the forest, and as proven by tonight's events, even the prince of Light would be hard-pressed to survive an unscheduled trek.

I held up a small orb that I'd brought to take us back to the Academy. There might not be a way out, but getting in was a bit easier if one has an established anchor. Mine was the dagger that Penne had given me during our first encounter. She didn't know it at the time, but I recognized that blade, or rather the workmanship. There was only one smithy who produced steel like that, and it was one used by Elites and Dreg-dwellers alike. I expected Penne was not one to often have much coin on her, so I wondered what she'd had to do in order to afford the weapon. I also noted some sort of emotional attachment to it, so I had kept it safe, fully intending to keep my word that I would hold onto it until she was ready to reclaim it.

I hoped that day would be soon.

Picturing the dagger in my mind, sitting where I had left it on my room's mantle, I connected to the Academy and the one thing that drew me there. I could have used anything for my anchor, but this made the spell effortless in a way that lit up my artifact in an instant. I was starting to care for the human, far more than I should have, and that frightened me more than anything my father could do to me. If I didn't convince Professor Surin that there was nothing amiss, he certainly would punish me—and Penne if she returned too late.

Because she would return to me.

I knew it in my bones.

A burst of Light sent me back to the Academy. I had intended to use the spell to bring both Penne and myself back. I didn't have a way to get to her now other than braving the forest if she returned to the Kingdom, but I couldn't wait to see if she'd find her way back. It was time for damage control.

Professor Surin burst into my room only moments after I had ported in. "What the frosted fae is going on?" he demanded.

Right on cue.

"Professor Surin," I drawled, caressing Penne's dagger to feel the fine engravings on the blade, "this is an unruly hour for you to visit. I thought we agreed to discuss matters in the morning?"

His curled ears twitched under long, silky hair. Golden motes grew and sparked around him like tiny explosions, telling me that whatever I had done had disrupted his magic.

Not good.

"You know very well why I'm here," he said, widening his eyes with an unspoken threat. "Your father did more than tell me to keep an eye on you. I am magically bound to report any suspicious activity." He held up a hand, showing me a ball of Light that writhed like a tortured creature. "Whatever you have done has created shockwaves in the very fabric of Light in this world. Tell me what's going on, or I'm going to have to rip it out of you."

Surin was one of the few fae with magic still in his veins that wasn't of royal lineage. He was ancient, one of the fae who had been a part of our old society, before Malice, before deceit and change. Which meant he was susceptible to being controlled by kings who had greater magic than he did.

Great.

Pretending to be unfazed, I ticked the tip of the dagger against my fang. He probably thought my lack of control over my canines a show of arrogance, but the truth was I was terrified. My fight or flight instinct overruled my ability to keep it cool, no matter how much of a good show I put on. "You can try, old fae, but you're just going to wear yourself out. I'm my father's son, after all."

The professor rubbed his temple. "Just tell me

what's going on. I really would prefer to retire for the evening instead of babysitting you."

"Fair enough." I pointed the dagger at a chair, to which Professor Surin took a seat. I sat adjacent from him and sighed. "Look, I didn't mean to use so much magic, but I was out at the breach my father had showed me a couple of weeks ago—"

"A breach?" Professor Surin asked, his eyes widening.

Interesting. My father had chosen to omit that rather important detail to his most trusted advisor.

"Yes, a breach," I reinforced, leaning in. "My father is growing more careless by the day. He is no longer fit to rule."

Professor Surin hummed in agreement. He might be my father's dog, but there was no denying that the King was slowly succumbing to the Malice he'd allowed into himself. Humans could commune with it, but fae, they either became dark or died once exposed. I feared either outcome. In death, fae society would pay even closer attention to what I was up to at the Academy. If he turned dark, well, that would open a whole other slew of problems I wasn't ready to deal with.

"That is why we are expediting the Queen's Class," Professor Surin said, crossing his arms.

"These girls all show promise. We don't have a year to pick the best one. I know you don't approve of such brutal tactics, but the Malice trials will find you the best bride capable of helping you take over your father's rule." His canines lengthened, a blatant show of aggression. "However, you are still yet the prince. Until such time of your inauguration, you will obey your father's rules. You know you're not permitted to leave Academy grounds without approval." He tilted his head. "Did you bring anyone with you?"

Blasted fae. The professor knew me too well.

I rolled my eyes, making a show of my impatience. "Do you think me a moron? I was just repairing a breach that would have encroached on *my* territory. I can be punished for my impertinence, if you wish, however I don't intend to allow the Kingdom to drown under Malice while my father takes his sweet time hoarding all of the Academy graduates in the Fae Realm." Doing Malice knows what over there.

Professor Surin nodded. "For now, I will suspend judgment. Your father returns in the morning and can make a decision for himself." He held up a finger as he turned to leave. "However, if any of the Candidates fail to show up for the Primary Exam results, any punishment I had in mind will pale in comparison."

I snorted in derision. "I would not be that stupid, Professor. Everyone will show up in the morning, as accounted for."

I clenched the hilt of Penne's dagger. I sure hoped that was true.

29

PENNE

Speech seemed lost to me, but that wasn't a problem. Steel made up for my stunned silence by babbling on how much I was going to love his Kingdom, his favorite shadow treats, a bit about his black cat named Midnight, and what dress I should wear for dinner.

"Don't look so glum," he said, pouting in a way that made him obnoxiously attractive. His eyes glittered with Malice, making him both sexy and terrifying. "I know it's a bit cramped keeping you in the castle, but once you're Queen, you'll be able to go wherever you want."

I jerked out of his grasp, not realizing that I'd been clinging to him this whole time. "Once I'm *what?*"

My panic was interrupted by a jingling to my left. I spun, ready to face whatever new horror had befallen me, only to find a full-sized Zizi grinning from ear to ear. She was even more beautiful in this form, complete with an onyx crown atop her head. "Penne!" she shouted and dove for me, hugging me around the middle. An icy chill of Malice invaded my body at her touch, causing my crown to retaliate. Unlike Steel, my body didn't seem to be able to process her variety of Malice. The surge of Light through my body made her flinch back. She gave a nervous chuckle, but didn't seem too put off. "I can't believe you're really here," she said, folding her hands in front of her and smoothing a long, silky black dress that glimmered with her movements.

She was breathtaking. I never would have imagined my dark magic pixie could have been a full-grown woman—or whatever she was. She wasn't exactly fae, but she certainly wasn't human."Zizi? You're…"

"Intruding," Steel offered with a terrifying glare. "Zizi, I told you that you could see her tomorrow."

Zizi propped her hands on her hips, causing her earrings to jingle again. "You might be King of the Underworld, but I'm Malice incarnate. Without *me* you're just a…" She twirled her hands.

"Creep?" I offered.

Zizi doubled over with a snort. "Oh, Penne! Yes! Creep!" She pointed at Steel as she descended into hysterical laughter. "Did you hear what she called you? It's hilarious… because it's true!"

Steel glared at both of us, looking thoroughly unamused. "She's just stunned from her realm travel." He laced his fingers through mine, bringing my hand up to his lips for a kiss. Butterflies exploded in my stomach and I found myself watching his every movement. It amazed me how I could go from fearing him to melting in a matter of seconds. This guy had some serious pull. "As my betrothed, you're allowed to call me whatever you wish, even if I've had others beheaded for less."

And we're back to fearing him.

Rubbing my eyes with my free hand, I sighed, then wavered on my feet as I tried to find a place to sit. We had been wandering around the ballroom, but it was a sleek onyx floor made for dancing, not sitting.

"You big brute," Zizi chided. "You can't just tell her she's your betrothed and meant to inherit the Malice throne just like that! Poor dear is about to faint."

Right, it had nothing to do with his poorly veiled threat.

Zizi moved to take my arm, then glanced at my crown and thought better of it. "Why don't you take her to her room? Give her some time to process."

The first logical thing I'd heard since coming here.

"But the dinner?" Steel pressed, his face falling. "And the dancing?"

Zizi shook her head. "No, sir. Not unless you want the whole Kingdom to see your future bride unconscious at your feet."

Steel didn't look like he was keen on parting with me anytime soon. He looked me over and his expression soured. Whatever he saw on my face convinced him that Zizi was right. "Fine. Perhaps I'm too eager." He tugged me along, walking at a brisk pace that made me feel dragged. "Off to bed, then. The sooner you rest, the sooner I can have your undivided attention. I'll have some food sent along and we can discuss our future in the morning."

"Do I get no say in this?" I said, finally finding my voice.

He flashed a grin, making me gasp as fiercely long fangs extended from his lips. I'd never seen a fae like this. "And what would you like to say?" he asked, whirling me into his arms as he began to dance. We'd exited the ballroom and now were in a long hall, but Steel didn't seem to care. He expertly guided me to a distant melody that appeared in my head, no doubt part of his power. "Is your first impression of me lacking?" He brought me in closer, his fingers slipping over the curve of my hip and his breath puffing against my face. Every touch gave me a thrill, but with it came a cold hint of Malice that my crown wanted to reject. My skin flashed with heat and his dark eyes glittered as if I'd challenged him. "It's not that Light fae, is it?" His grin faded as his voice lowered. "Lucas."

I cleared my throat, then swallowed, suddenly finding my tongue too dry. "No, of course not." I'd been plotting Lucas's death only hours ago.

I'd also kissed him.

And liked it.

Steel's eyes narrowed as his fingers on me tightened. "You don't have to lie to me, darling." He tapped his temple. "I can still hear your thoughts, you know."

Crap.

"Then why ask me anything at all?" I snapped, not appreciating the invasion of privacy. It was one thing when he was a voice in my head, but now he was a tall, handsome fae who was making absurd proclamations that I was to be his bride in a realm I hadn't even known existed. "You seem to have everything planned out for me, anyway."

He frowned and ran a finger through my hair, brushing the blonde strand off my shoulder. "I can only hear your thoughts when you shout them at me. It's our Malice bond, darling. Once you learn to control it—once I teach you everything I know—you'll be able to keep your thoughts secret, if that is your wish." He took the long strand he'd been stroking and kissed it, making my defenses weaken a little. "As for my plans, I only speak of destiny. You and I were chosen to be together by Malice itself. I've waited for you all your life. I can wait a little longer."

I didn't understand what he meant until I caught his gaze going to my chest. I ran my fingers over my raised Malice scar.

Had my bonding been more than an unfortunate accident? Had I really been chosen by Malice to be the Queen of this realm?

No, it was way too much to process. And even if that was true, Malice had destroyed my world. Sure, I might have found a way to co-exist with it, even use it to my advantage, but I could never love *Malice.*

I had to get out of here.

Hurt crossed Steel's expression, but if he'd heard that thought, he didn't comment on it. "Your chambers are this way, sweetheart. You've had a long day, and as much as Zizi gets on my nerves, she tends to be right about these things. We'll discuss our future in the morning."

He waited until I offered a shaky nod, then took me to a room that put the luxurious accommodations at the Academy to shame. I had to blink a few times at the burst of color after so much shadow and glittering darkness. Malice still lingered like black diamonds in the floors and the wall, but the room sparkled with clarity and a rainbow of color that lifted my spirits. The room boasted an emerald-toned couch, a bed with floral pattern sheets, drapes of red velvet, and a carpeted floor with a delicious cream that looked like dessert icing so soft I didn't even want to walk on it.

"It's beautiful," I said on an intake of breath.

Steel beamed. "I thought you might like it." He gave me a nudge. "Just because you're the Malice Princess doesn't mean you have to limit yourself to dismal colors, although black does look good on you." He splayed both hands and lifted his chin. "See? I can be accommodating." He bowed, then blew me a kiss. "I'll have many more surprises for you tomor-row, sweetheart. Food will arrive shortly. Eat, relax, sleep, and know that you're safe here."

I curled my fingers over the head of a desk chair and nodded. "If you say so."

I'd never felt safe a day in my life. I certainly wasn't going to start now.

When Steel left me alone and closed the door, I expelled the breath I'd been holding. Without his presence pressing in all around me, I felt like I could think clearly. Something about him was both intoxi-cating and deafening.

King of Malice, I remembered Zizi saying. If he was a royal fae, and linked to me through my Malice scar, then it made sense. He had power over me, and that could be dangerous.

My initial thought came to the surface that I needed to escape. I felt out of place in a world of Malice wearing a glittering pink dress and a tiny golden crown atop my head. The adornment had been surprisingly quiet during my exchange with the dark fae, but I had just used an enormous amount of Light to travel realms, so perhaps it was still stunned.

Holy fae... Realm travel.

"Okay, Penne. Keep it together," I said to myself

as I paced the long room. The creamy carpet sank underneath my steps, but I wouldn't be lulled into a sense of security by menial comforts. Steel had planned this. He was dark fae. That meant he was dangerous.

I had been marked as a child, unwittingly betrothed to the Malice King and turned into prey to be pounced on the moment my defenses were down. Had he known that I would need Light to travel to his world? Most likely. Perhaps it was why he'd encouraged me to take the crown. He had known it would bond to me and set me on a path that would lead me to him.

I gripped the tiny crown at my head. "Laurel, are you in there?" I didn't know who to turn to, but perhaps if Malice wasn't on my side anymore, Light would be.

Silence.

I ground my teeth together. "There's got to be something!" Frustration brought me to my knees and I slammed my fists to the ground, the impact muffled by the carpet. The impact popped an object from my dress cleavage and I stared at it.

Holy fae, thank you, Olli!

I'd totally forgotten about the artifact she'd given me. Now I was grateful my stupid dress didn't have pockets. The Malice King probably would have searched those if he'd thought I would have a means of escape.

Frantic, I snatched up the disc and stared at it.

"Come on!"

Nothing happened at first, then my Light slowly reacted to the artifact and warmed my skin. Olli had found it in a locked room owned by a powerful Light Fae, which meant this thing had to have some punch.

I squeezed my eyes shut. "Concentrate. Focus, Penne. Keep it together."

I took in a deep breath, held it, then slowly let it out. The warmth in my body grew and connected to the disc, building until the icy touch of Malice eased away. This wouldn't be like my travel to the Malice Realm, wild and uncontrolled. I needed to know where I was going, which meant I needed an anchor to focus on.

Lucas.

He was the first thing to pop into my head. Maybe it was dumb, but I went with it and thought about how he made me feel. How I knew I should fear him, should wish him dead like all the other fae just for what he was, but one glance from his silver eyes disarmed me. They say the eyes are the window to the soul, and he was the first person in my life not to have emptiness in them. When he looked at me, really looked at me, I saw him for who he really was.

And he wasn't evil.

Maybe he was a jerk, a perv, and irresponsible for landing me here in the first place, but I'd kick his butt later. For now, all I wanted was to get out of here, and perhaps explore the mysterious connection I had with the prince of the Light fae.

Magic reacted to my inner desires, pulling power from the artifact in my grasp as a brilliant flash exploded behind my eyes, and then I felt myself propelled through realms straight to him.

Straight to Lucas.

IT WAS ONLY my second time traveling realms, so I figured I could be forgiven for my lack of control when it came to the landing.

Lucas was my anchor, which gave me a direction to work towards unlike my first travel where Steel had yanked me through. This time I wanted to leave. I wanted to find Lucas and explore the connection between us.

Time and space ripped apart in a grand shredding of Light and Malice. I saw him, Lucas, waiting for me as he stared at an open flame of his hearth contemplating something that glinted in his hand.

My dagger.

"Lucas!" I shouted as I fell into my home realm, relishing that I'd done it all on my own. I didn't need some Malice King to tell me how to use my magic. I was strong enough on my own.

My pride was short-lived as I barreled head-first into Lucas, sending us sprawling to the floor. He hit the wall hard, luckily missing the fireplace.

The dagger went flying, a flash of steel in the air as it flung across the room. Lucas wrapped his arms around me and caught his breath. By the way he wheezed, I'd hit him pretty hard. "Penne, holy fae, you scared the living Light out of me."

I peered up at him only to find him grinning. His smile was soft this time, a gentle curve to his canines —as he perpetually seemed unable to control them— as he gazed down at me. He brushed aside a strand of my wild hair and my crown flashed my body with fresh heat.

Finally! Laurel shouted in my head. *I was smothered in that terrible realm. Stifled, constrained!*

I smirked as she released a litany of complaints. "My crown is complaining it didn't like the Malice realm," I informed Lucas when he gave me a raised brow.

He grinned. "I would imagine not." He squeezed me, surprising me by his blatant elation that I was still alive. "I'm so glad you're back. Don't do that to me again, okay?"

I chuckled. "What, disappear to the Malice Realm? Don't worry, won't be happening again." I decided it best to leave out the part of my betrothal to the Malice King. I hadn't heard his voice in my head ever since I'd bonded with the crown, so as long as I left it on, I should be safe from him.

That's right! Laurel chimed. *Guess you're stuck with me!*

Untangling myself from Lucas, I stood and brushed myself off with a sigh. I wasn't too keen on the idea of remaining a pretty pink princess for the rest of my life, but until I found a better solution, Laurel would get her way.

"Professor Surin was here less than an hour ago," Lucas said, carefully getting to his feet as he rubbed at his side where I'd catapulted into him. "I covered for you, but if you're not back in your room when he checks in, I'm never going to hear the end of it."

His smirk was an effort to put me at ease, but I saw the fear in his eyes. He needed our secrets to remain hidden until he was ready to face the professor and his father.

I'd never been in his room before, so I didn't exactly know how to get back to mine. "Is it far?"

He chuckled. "Yes, but don't worry about that. I'll teleport you."

I nodded. Even though I'd had my fair share of teleportation for the day, it would be the safest way to get me back. "Very well. And then tomorrow? What's the plan?"

A mischievous glint flashed in his eyes as he retrieved the dagger, then handed it to me. "You're going to need this."

I took the blade, relishing how it weighed perfectly in my grip. I'd forgotten how much I'd missed it as I ran my thumb over the flat edge. "So, I've convinced you I know how to wield a weapon?"

He chuckled. "I know exactly who you are, Malice Caster of the Northern Sector, and what you're capable of."

My blood ran cold at the blatant reveal. "So, what happens next?"

He handed me an artifact and it hummed with magic, ready to teleport me back to my room. My world began to spin as his words followed me.

"We bring the whole system down."

*A*ll this time, Lucas and I had been on the same page. Why hadn't he just told me he hated the Academy just as much as I did? Maybe he thought I wouldn't believe him, but I was pretty good at telling when someone was lying. Lucas harbored a hatred towards his own people that shone as clear as day when he opened up to me like that. I wanted to ask him why... What had festered such resentment against those he's supposed to call family?

If he thought I couldn't relate to that, then he hadn't looked into my history. Orphaned. Sold. Abandoned. However I looked at it, my family didn't exist.

Olli screamed when I teleported back into the

room and flung herself into my arms. "I thought you were gone for good!" she sobbed.

Stunned, I patted the back of her head. "Uh, there, there. I'm all right."

She peeled herself away from me. "Don't ever do that to me again!" She sniffled, then plucked a tiny square handkerchief from her apron. I found myself jealous of the pocketed attire. At least she didn't have to store objects in her breasts. "When I checked back in on you, you'd disappeared without a trace, and I know you hadn't left the room, because I was waiting outside the entire time."

"What?" I asked, one of my eyebrows shooting up. "I thought you were going to scope out the other Candidates?"

She blew out a breath and dabbed her nose with the cloth. "I just didn't want you to feel awkward that I was waiting outside. You asked me to leave, remember? Is that because you were trying to escape?" Her eyes widened. "Did you? Why did you come back?"

The innocent pleading in her eyes said she hoped it was because of our friendship, but in truth I'd forgotten about her. "I thought you liked it here," I said, lowering my voice. Guilt washed over me. Had I gotten Olli all wrong?

She sniffled again. "That was before I heard Professor Surin whisper with Lady Rita about the Primary Exam results. Did you know that you've already been scored? And the results are expedited?"

"What does that mean?"

She swallowed and glanced at the door as if someone might burst in at any moment. "It means there's only going to be one graduate tomorrow."

One graduate…

One survivor.

Crap.

IT TOOK AN EXTENDED EFFORT, but I got Olli to calm down, even after Professor Surin surprised us with a visit. He seemed taken aback to see me and mumbled his apology for intruding and wished me luck for the Primary Exam.

Lucas had been right. The old fae was onto us.

The next day, we all gathered at the main audience hall, only to be greeted by a somber-looking Lady Rita.

The six other girls stood in a semi-circle assorted by our rainbow colors. Melinda gave me her usual glare while Rylie quietly stood at my side,

her hand finding mine to give a squeeze of encouragement.

"Today is the day, my lovely Crown Princess
Candidates," Lady Rita said, straightening as she
surveyed us. "The day a Crown Princess is revealed."

A wave of excitement swept through the small
gathering, followed by more than one glance at
Melinda. She beamed, no doubt thinking she most
definitely would be graduating.

Good luck.

"Settle down, now. We must make our way to the
teleportation room and greet the King upon his
return." She gathered her skirts. "This way."

The teleportation room?

My stomach dropped.

Lucas was nowhere to be seen as we marched in
a quiet line behind Lady Rita's bobbing form.
Golden magic glided over her skin, making her look
like a beacon of the group. We reached a door and
she swept it open with a wave of her hand, revealing
a long walkway far above the Academy grounds. A
single spire waited for us on the other side.

A rare glimpse of the other students at Crown
Princess Academy awarded itself as they gathered on
the lower levels to watch us. They peered up in awe
and waved little colored flags. I frowned when I

spotted a surplus of red and realized they had placed bets on which one of us would graduate.

"It's a tradition," Rylie informed me, keeping her voice low. "They don't know what it's really like being in the Queen's Class," she added, noting the rage making my jaw spasm.

"I would hope not," I ground out. I had a feeling that most of us were marching straight to our deaths, had Lucas and I not had a plan up our sleeves. Or in my case, frills. The pressure of my trusty dagger strapped to my waist gave me confidence. This was going to end, here and now. None of these girls were going to die on my watch.

Even Melinda? Zizi chimed in my head. *I mean, you can't be expected to save alllll of the Candidates. If one shouldn't make it, well, that's on the fae, am I right?*

I smirked. Leave it to Zizi to make me feel better at a time like this.

Lady Rita snapped her fingers and the breeze caught a spell she mumbled under her breath. A thud hit my chest as the doors to the spire parted and revealed a room with no windows. She ushered us in and closed the doors behind us, leaving my eyes to adjust to the dim surroundings.

Fae magic illuminated walls and columns decorated with elaborate engravings. Like everything with the fae, nothing was bland and everything was overdone. A large arch framed a permanent portal in the center of the room and boasted a wavering veil. I tried to focus on the watery surface, but couldn't make out what was on the other side.

"Only the Queen's Class and those who have graduated with honors are permitted in this room," Lady Rita said, smiling and straightening with pride. As a graduate of ten years, she no doubt thought of herself highly to be included in that number. "The King will be arriving any moment, so look lively." She clapped, making us straighten our backs.

"Get ready to bow to me," Melinda hissed, stabbing me in the rib with a manicured fingernail.

I flinched, my instincts wanting to break the offending finger, but I decided against it.

We'll see who's bowing to whom, missy! Zizi shouted in my head.

You're very loud, Laurel complained, her jingling tones making me rub my ears. *I don't think I like this marriage of Malice and Light. Penne, do we have to keep her?*

"Both of you, shut it," I whispered through clenched teeth.

If I thought I was knee-deep in crazy before, now I was certain of it.

"What was that, Candidate Penelope?" Lady Rita asked, clearly unamused with me. She'd been giving us instructions while voices had been bickering inside my head.

Melinda smirked. "Pink Penelope was bragging, Lady Rita. But I really don't think being slutty with the prince is going to get her any extra marks, right? Or is that the kind of Academy we're enrolled in?"

Lady Rita's lips twitched. "Prince Lucas can hear you, Candidate Melinda. I would be careful with your words."

All the girls searched the room. I suddenly realized how many shadows were in this place among the spirals and elaborate decoration. The prince slipped out of one of them, his canines extended in a grin.

Melinda went pale.

The prince might be a creature of Light magic, but he was just as good as me at hiding in plain sight. I would have laughed out loud, but I knew better. I had to play my part until this was over, and then send all these poor girls home. Melinda was just a product of her environment. A snobby, cruel, pathetic environment.

Lucas cleared his throat. "You only say that because I turned you down, *Candidate* Melinda,"

Lucas said, eliciting a chuckle from the other girls. "If sleeping with me would have earned you another golden ticket, I have no doubt that you would have done it."

"She would have done it regardless," murmured Catherine as she lifted a hand adorned with far too many emerald rings to match her dress.

"That's quite enough," Lady Rita snipped as she stepped away from the portal that had begun to shimmer. "The King will be here any moment and I would appreciate if we could all greet him in cordial fashion."

Lucas gave the professor a solemn nod. It amazed me how he seemed so cool and collected, like his typical pompous self and not at all like a fae about to ignite an act of treason. I shifted my stance, comforted by the weight of steel over my thigh that promised me I hadn't dreamed all of it up. Lucas and I were on the same page. We were going to bring the whole system down.

Doubt crept in when the King emerged from the portal, followed by an entourage of beautiful women that wore glittering tiaras. They didn't look silly like the Queen's Class. They were refined, elegant, and dripped with Light magic as if they'd taken a bath in the stuff. Lucas was just as mesmerized as the rest of us with the gathering.

"Son," the King said, clapping Lucas on the back with a jovial smile. He'd been so serious all this time that I hardly recognized the white-haired fae. He still struck me as elderly in appearance, but joy sparked in his eyes that had been dull before. Perhaps his return to the fae realm had done him some much-needed good.

"Father," Lucas replied, his tone was kind but I sensed the tension in his stance. He stared at the women, taking in their golden glow that basked the spire's room with their beauty. "Who have you brought with you?"

The King barked a laugh. "Why, these are the previous graduates of the Queen's Class."

My eyes widened and Lucas dared a glance in my direction. I knew the same thoughts were going through both our minds. Had we misunderstood? Would all of the graduates survive?

"You ladies knew my mother?" Lucas asked as one thumb hooked into his pants pocket. He was trying to be casual, but I knew he was on the verge of pulling out of our agreement depending on what we heard today.

"Yes," one woman answered, stepping forward as

she brushed her brilliant ruby hair from her shoulder. Her fingers dripped with diamonds and she positively glowed with magic. Even her eyes looked like tiny gems that glittered with enough power that explained why she looked so young, even though she was likely older than Lucas and I combined. "My name is Fiona. Your mother was a lovely girl. I'm so sorry to have heard of her passing."

The grief in her tone was genuine, as was the surprise. "You didn't know?" Lucas asked, this time his voice pitching at the end. "How is it that I never knew about you ladies? Or that you didn't know of my mother's passing?"

She chuckled. "We've been doing our work all these years in another realm." She glanced at the King. "If I may be permitted to share that information?"

He nodded. "It's about time my son knew the truth, as should this new selection of Queen's Class Candidates." He took a wider stance and met each of our gazes one by one. "Malice grows ever stronger and it has begun to invade more worlds than just our own. There are seven realms, three of which thrive on Light. The Human Realm, the Fae Realm, and..." He took a deep breath, "the realm of the gods."

The girls gasped with Rylie being the first to

blurt a question. "The gods? Really? Have you met them? The true deities?"

Lady Rita hissed at Rylie. "Hush, girl! Know your place."

The King waved a hand. "It's quite all right. It's hard to believe, I'm sure. But this is precisely why I have extracted our secret weapon from the gods' realm. We need the graduates of the Queen's Class now more than ever, as well as a new Queen to establish the royal line with my son." He straightened. "Now that you know the prize that awaits you, whether you graduate as the Crowned Queen or not, you have a vital place in fae society. Let's move on to the results of the Primary Exam."

"Results?" Hannah asked, smoothing her purple dress. "But we haven't taken the exam yet."

The King laughed. "Oh, my dear, what do you think you'd been doing these past two weeks? I have asked Lucas and Professor Surin to watch all of you and assign appropriate scores." He clapped his hands. "Now, where is the professor?"

Lucas cleared his throat. "Otherwise occupied, unfortunately. It was a rather grave matter involving the... issue we addressed before your departure, father. But not to worry, he shared his score with me."

The breach? Why would professor Surin be off grounds to deal with that? And I knew for a fact that I had dealt with the Malice that had encroached on Kingdom and Dreg territory. No, Lucas was up to something and he'd somehow roped the professor in on it.

The King frowned, but nodded after considering the situation. "Very well." He extended a hand. "Proceed with your judgment."

Lucas cleared his throat and surveyed my class. The girls straightened, all of them looking nervous— including Melinda. I'd been hiding in my room throughout the past two weeks, so I wasn't sure what kind of scores the other girls could expect. In fact, I wasn't sure why Lucas had made such an effort sabotaging my performances if he was just going to take over the final scores anyway.

Lucas produced an artifact which he activated with a bolt of Light. It projected an illusion into the air, showing Rylie and me in the Music Hall. I knew for a fact that if this was to be our score, I would pass with flying colors. Rylie's music came through beautiful, a melody with hypnotic tones flooded the small room and lit a smile across my face. I wanted Rylie to be recognized for her talent. She had almost died that first day just because the fae had an idea of what power meant, but Rylie had a different kind of power. She had the ability to feel, and in a world where suffering ruled and so many people shut off their emotions, that was something special indeed.

Then, I started to sing. I wasn't ashamed of my voice. I had quite a nice one, in fact. It was one of the few traits I liked about myself, even if I didn't enjoy singing except when I could muffle my room so no one could hear me. Nothing quite said "terrifying Malice Caster" like a blonde with a penchant for music.

But the voice that came out wasn't my own. I cringed at the unpleasant off-tone. So, this was his sabotage. Was he trying to humiliate me?

I attempted to match his gaze, but he wouldn't look at me as he played the clip. Even when Melinda delighted in a not-so-secret chuckle behind her hand and my cheeks turned red.

"Candidate Penelope, score zero in musical talent. Candidate Rylie, score three."

The King hummed in agreement and I realized that he would not have blindly accepted Lucas's score without seeing the results for himself, especially without Professor Surin. Lucas went through each trial: music, weaponry, and the greenhouse with scores for every student, making sure to give me zero marks with the appropriate humiliating evidence. By the end of it, I wanted to throw myself across the room and strangle him. I clenched my fists and locked my knees as one of the elegant graduates poured raw Malice into champagne glasses. Lucas went around the room, offering golden slips equivalent to the scores provided. I glanced at Rylie, worried that she'd only gotten three. Even if her musical score had been excellent, she hadn't been able to impress Lucas or the King.

I cursed myself internally. This was my fault. I should have been there for her instead of hiding in my room.

As if she could read my thoughts, she shook her head. She would never blame me. I knew that, but it didn't lessen the sting that she'd been put in danger I could have prevented.

"It's time for your finals," the King said, all mirth gone from his voice. No matter how much hope he'd dangled that there could be more than one graduate from the Queen's Class, it was clear that we were all in very real danger. Even Melinda looked uneasy as she accepted her flute and plunked her golden slips into it, the high score barely enough to take out the sharp black of the liquid. Her hand began to shake, sloshing the liquid in the glass. One of the graduates reached out to steady her.

"This is your final test. This dose of Malice is significant enough to awaken the Light in your bodies and turn you near-immortal. Do not fear it. Embrace this gift," the King said, spreading his arms with grandeur.

I looked to Lucas if he was going to act. I had my dagger, but I couldn't take on the King and his lackeys. Those girls had enough magic in them to wipe the Kingdom off the map. I had a feeling the King knew Lucas was up to something and had brought reinforcements to make sure things went smoothly.

So far, it seemed to be working.

When none of us moved to take our drinks, most still bubbling with the golden slips that had been dropped in, the King snorted in derision. "Fiona," he snapped.

She immediately responded by flicking her wrist. A compulsion took over me and I brought the flute to my lips. My nostrils flared as the metallic scent of Malice took over my senses. This was a concentrated dose, and most likely fatal without enough Light to dilute it. I had my crown and Laurel, but I didn't think that would be enough.

Lucas finally glanced at me and a flash of worry

crossed his gaze. Good, he still cared. I was starting to wonder.

He flicked his wrist and heat spread up my thigh where my dagger was strapped to my skin. I sucked in a breath and could have kissed him. Of course! He'd infused my dagger with Light. He wasn't going to abandon me. This had been his plan all along.

Some of the girls had an intense dose to deal with, Gem being one of them. She gave in to the compulsion first and downed the vile drink with a grimace. She choked, then tossed the glass to the ground to shatter as she screamed. She crashed to her knees and black tendrils of magic laced over her skin, breaking her bones with audible snaps as she cried black tears.

Melinda's eyes widened, but if anything the display made her more determined to win. She took her drink to her lips and drank it down until it was finished. She flinched as the Malice shot through her body, but she fought back with a surge of Light. She glanced at me. "I'm going to win," she said, her words a command. "Drink your Malice and die so there's one less pitiful Candidate for me to contend with."

Charming.

I found Lucas again and he gave me a slight nod.

I would have to trust him. He wasn't going to let me die from an undiluted glass of Malice.

Right?

I hoped so.

With a leap of faith, I took my fill, and embraced the worst pain of my life.

31

LUCAS

She would survive.

She had to survive.

I repeated the mantra in my mind over and over again until I watched Penne drink her Malice. Every fibre of my being screamed for me to stop her. I couldn't understand how my father could watch all of this so calmly, much less the other members of the Queen's Class who'd graduated with my mother. They stood by while each girl took her Malice with resignation, accepting what fate may come, even if it would be death.

Perhaps they didn't react because they'd seen this before. They'd watched their fellow Candidates succumb to Malice and die.

Screams overtook the small chamber and I

resisted the urge to clamp my hands over my ears. It was my fault I didn't have a better plan. These girls had to go through this. Penne had to use their suffering, as well as her own, before she could end a centuries-long tradition.

I just hoped she could figure that out before it killed them all.

Penne's eyes went wide as the Malice took over. Her once blue eyes that I loved so much clouded over with pitch until her gaze was nothing but darkness. She threw her head back as she released an otherworldly scream, one that writhed with the agony of a lifetime of surviving Malice and pain. I had activated the Light in her dagger, a small boost against a tidal wave of evil.

Flickers of gold hinted around her form and I held my breath, hoping it would be enough of an edge to get her through this transition. The other girls worked to extinguish the Malice they'd just ingested, but not Penne. Every trial where she'd taken Malice into herself she'd held onto it—and now she would use it to her advantage.

I knew the moment when it came.

So did my father.

"What is this?" he shouted, recognizing the writhing power of Light and Malice that stitched itself together in Penne's soul. She staggered to her feet and growled at the fae, raw primal rage that would shred him apart if I allowed it.

A part of me wanted to. My father didn't deserve to live after what he'd done to my mother, but there was a greater use for Penne's power.

"The portal!" I shouted, then ran to her and yanked her by the wrist. The once fragile human now pulled back from me, far stronger as she pushed me to the ground with a heavy blow to my ribs. I expelled a lungful of air as tears sprang to my eyes. "Penne!" I pleaded. "You have to target the portal! Stop this from happening ever again!"

The girls around her were dying, save maybe Melinda who stared open-mouthed as she still worked to eliminate the Malice within herself. She looked like she wanted to kill Penne, but she was thankfully too occupied with her own dose of Malice to do anything but growl.

The others, though, writhed and died around us. Tendrils of darkness sprouted from them like vines and sprawled towards Penne, adding to her chaotic power. It needed a target or she was going to implode.

Something in those midnight eyes flashed with

recognition and she turned from my father who balked with horror.

She held out a hand, blackness and Light writhing around her fingers, as she focused on the flickering surface of the portal.

"This is for humanity," she whispered as a life-time of suffering and rage exploded from the Malice scar on her chest, crashing into the portal and sending an ear-splitting blast cascading throughout the realm.

It was finished.

EPILOGUE
STEEL

"I told you she'd do it," Zizi said.

I adjusted the reigns to my Malice horse, a beast that was more shadow and bones than living creature. "This was not how I pictured it when you said Penne would bring me to her realm."

I had envisioned a courtship, time together where she would fall for me and recognize how I'd always been there all her life as an invaluable piece of her soul. Instead, she'd blocked me out, accepted the Light and that ridiculous pink dress her precious Lucas made her wear.

Now she'd nearly died, accepted the marriage of Light and Malice in order to rip a hole through a permanent portal meant to connect the Light fae world to the human one. Perhaps she thought she could close it, but that's not how portals worked.

When one door closes, another one opens.

A brilliant emerald forest spread out before me, surrounding a whitewashed castle that smoked with the remnants of Penne's work that had brought me here. She's also more than destabilized the barrier that the fae had put up around their precious Kingdom and darkness greedily sprawled in. It wouldn't be long before the entire place drowned in it.

Penne might not have invited me on purpose, but she'd still done the one thing that could bring us together.

I clicked my tongue and sent my horse into the forest, smirking as the creatures within scurried away from us. I was the King of Malice, and Zizi at my side was Malice incarnate, so they knew better than to challenge us.

I sensed Penne at the end of this trail. I was a patient dark fae, and I would give her the space she needed before winning her over.

This time, she had nowhere to run.

This time, she would be mine.

Thank you for reading! Do you want to see what happens next? Be sure to read Crown Princess Academy: Book Two!

Thank you for reading the first installment of Crown Princess Academy! Keep reading Penne's story in Crown Princess Academy: Book Two!

Please take a moment to leave a review on Amazon and help A.J. to reach more readership. It doesn't have to be much! "Loved it!" will do!

Be sure to join the A.J. Newsletter to be informed of new releases by heading on over to AJ-Flowers.com!

Printed in Great Britain
by Amazon

79861558R00192